Sky Hawk

Gill Lewis

OXFORD
UNIVERSITY PRESS

OXFORD

UNIVERSITY PRESS

Great Clarendon Street, Oxford OX2 6DP

Oxford University Press is a department of the University of Oxford.
It furthers the University's objective of excellence in research, scholarship,
and education by publishing worldwide in

Oxford   New York

Auckland   Cape Town   Dar es Salaam   Hong Kong   Karachi
Kuala Lumpur   Madrid   Melbourne   Mexico City   Nairobi
New Delhi   Shanghai   Taipei   Toronto

With offices in

Argentina   Austria   Brazil   Chile   Czech Republic   France   Greece
Guatemala   Hungary   Italy   Japan   Poland   Portugal   Singapore
South Korea   Switzerland   Thailand   Turkey   Ukraine   Vietnam

Oxford is a registered trade mark of Oxford University Press
in the UK and in certain other countries

British Library Cataloguing in Publication Data
Data available

ISBN: 978-0-19-275624-4

5 7 9 10 8 6 4

Printed in Great Britain

Paper used in the production of this book is a natural,
recyclable product made from wood grown in sustainable forests.
The manufacturing process conforms to the environmental
regulations of the country of origin.

and is so engaging it almost turns the pages for you.'
Michael Morpurgo

'Rich in atmosphere and full of heart, Sky Hawk
is an intense and touching story . . . A book to treasure.'
Lovereading4kids.com

'A heart-soaring read.'
The Big Issue

'An edge-of-your-seat wildlife adventure that tells a very
human ory of friendship, discovery and an incredible journey. I loved it!'
Kate Humble, Presenter of BBC's Springwatch

'A ?   noving and inspiring tale of wildlife, friendship and growing up.'
TBK Magazine

Lewis shows beautifully how there is always hope in sadness.'
Literary Review

'This   autifully written, captivating book should be on everyone's bookcase.
Breathtaking. Poignant. Unforgettable.'
Virginia McKenna, Founder of the Born Free Foundation

'The reader is held spellbound by the intensity of the writing and the
optimism in the message. This is a book for everyone from 8 to 80+!'
The School Librarian

'Sky Hawk is a book almost as incredible as the ospreys it is written about; with vivid descriptions that have made this book my new favourite. It is like a Michael Morpurgo novel, containing brilliant characterisation, as well as much more. I love how the osprey makes and breaks friendships. I couldn't ask for more in a book.'

ARTHUR, AGE 12

'I really enjoyed reading Sky Hawk. Some parts had me sitting up straight in my bed eager to read more. All of the characters were believable and realistic. Iona's and Callum's friendship for each other and loyalty for Iris is really special.'

MILLIE, AGE 11

'I was totally absorbed by this wonderful book which was full of many happy and sad moments. The book taught me lots about the life of the osprey and at times, I felt as though I was in the story too. I would recommend this book to children aged ten and up, particularly if they are nature lovers, but not afraid to shed a tear! Marks out of ten: eleven!'

HARRY, AGE 10

'Sky Hawk is a gripping story. Gill Lewis captures you and sweeps you to the Scottish countryside. When I read this book, it made me feel like I was standing there with Callum and Iona next to me, watching the nest. The ending was very beautiful. I would recommend this book to anyone aged 10 and up, especially animal lovers.'

ELISE, AGE 11

For

Roger

Georgie, Bethany and Jemma

and for

Huw

who still walks with me across the mountains

Prologue

The pattern of this landscape is folded deep, deep within her memory. She rides the currents of air that curl like rapids over the mountains. Below, the lochs reflect the cloud and sunlight. They lie in the valleys like scattered fragments of fallen sky. The cold north wind carries the remembered scent of pine and heather. The ice-carved valleys guide her.

She is coming.

CHAPTER 1

I saw her first, a pale skinny girl lying on a flat rock below the rapids. She was leaning out over the edge, reaching down into a deep pool of still water. Swirls of river foam clung to the bottom of her rolled-up sleeves and the floating ends of her long red hair. She was watching something in the dark river-shadows.

Rob and Euan pulled up beside me by the gap in the trees, their bike tyres skidding on the muddy track.

'What you looking at, Callum?' said Rob.

'Someone's down there,' I said, 'a girl.'

Euan pushed away a pine branch to get a better view down to the river. 'Who is it?'

'Dunno,' I said. 'She's nuts though. It must be freezing in there.' I looked up and down the river to see if she was with anyone, but there was no one. She was on her own.

The river was fast and swollen from the heavy rains. It came down from the loch in the high glen above us. Late March snow still clung to the mountain gullies. The loch and river were cold as ice.

'She's on our river,' scowled Rob.

The girl slipped her arm in deeper. Water crept over her sleeve and up to her shoulder.

'What's she doing?' I said.

Euan dropped his bike onto the ground. 'Fishing, that's what.'

The girl plunged forwards in a blur of spray. When she sat back up, she was clutching a massive brown trout. It flapped and thrashed in her wet hands. She flicked her hair back over her head, and for the first time we could clearly see her face.

'I know her,' said Rob.

I turned to look at him. His face was dark and grim.

'Who is she?' I said.

But Rob was already off his bike and marching down the riverbank towards her.

'Rob,' I called.

The girl looked up and saw us, and tried to hide the fish in her arms. Euan and I ran down to the water's edge following Rob. A narrow channel of fast water ran between us and the girl.

Rob yelled across at her. 'Iona McNair!'

The girl scrambled to her feet.

Rob leapt across to the flat rock and grabbed her arm. 'You're a thief, Iona McNair, just like your ma.'

The girl struggled to hold the slippery fish. 'I'm not stealing,' she cried.

Rob pulled the fish off her and jumped back onto the riverbank. 'Then what d'you call this?' He held the fish up high. 'This is Callum's river and you're stealing.'

They all looked at me now.

'What about it, Callum?' said Rob. 'What's the punishment for fishing on your farm without a permit?'

I opened my mouth but no words came out.

'I don't need a permit,' spat Iona, 'I didn't use a rod.'

'You're a thief,' shouted Rob. 'And we don't want you here.'

I looked at Iona and she narrowed her eyes at me.

Rob dropped the thrashing fish on the ground and picked up a plastic bag next to Iona's coat on the riverbank. 'What else have you got in here?'

'Leave it, it's mine,' yelled Iona.

Rob tipped out a pair of old trainers and a tatty notebook.

He picked up the notebook from the ground and flicked the mud from it.

Iona jumped across to the riverbank and tried to snatch it from him. 'Give it back. It's secret.' She bit her lip, as if she'd said too much.

Her hands were shaking, and her arms and feet were blue with cold.

'Give it back, Rob,' I said.

'Yeah,' said Euan. 'Come on, Rob, let's go.'

'Wait a sec,' said Rob. He started flicking over the pages. 'Let's see what secret she's trying to hide.'

Iona tried to grab the book, but Rob held it out of reach, laughing.

'What's your secret, Iona McNair?' he taunted.

The pages fluttered in the breeze. I glimpsed pencil drawings of animals and birds, and lots of scribbled notes. A page hung open on a painting of the loch in deep greys and purples.

Iona jumped and tore the book from his hands. She leapt across to the flat rock and held the book over the water. 'I'll never tell you,' she cried, 'never.'

Rob took a step towards her. 'Come on. Let's see.'

Iona's face was fierce and set.

'Leave it, Rob,' I shouted.

Sky Hawk

Euan tried to pull him away, but Rob shook him off.

'What's the big secret, Iona?' shouted Rob. He lunged towards her.

Iona leapt across the rocks to the far riverbank. It was an impossible leap. She slipped on wet rock and went tumbling into a deep pool on the far side. The notebook flew from her hand and spun through the air before it hit the fast-water and was gone. Iona scrambled out of the river and disappeared up the steep bank into dense pine forest. The river surged down the valley between us, taking the notebook and Iona's secret away down with it.

CHAPTER 2

Euan turned on Rob. 'What d'you do that for? It was three against one. She was on her own.'

Rob kicked the heather and stared at the far riverbank. 'My dad lost his business because of her ma.' He turned, grim-faced, to Euan. 'She stole every last bit of his money and ran off. She wouldn't dare put a foot in Scotland again.'

'That was years ago,' I said. 'What's Iona doing back here now?'

'Stealing for her ma probably,' snapped Rob. 'They're a bad lot, the McNairs. My dad will never forgive that family for what she did.'

Euan spat on the ground and glared at Rob. 'What'll you do with that fish?'

Sky Hawk

Rob picked up the trout. It was dead. Its body had lost its bright sheen and its eyes were dull and glassy. He turned to me and shoved it in my deep coat pocket. 'It's your river, so it's your fish.'

'I don't want it,' I said.

But Rob just scowled at me and marched up to the bikes. 'She's left her coat and trainers,' I said to Euan.

'Best leave them,' he said, following Rob. 'She'll find them on her way back.'

Euan cycled off behind Rob, and I watched them skid and bump down the muddy track.

I pulled my hood up, clipped my cycle helmet over the top and stuffed my hands into my gloves. I looked up and down the far riverbank to see if I could catch a glimpse of the girl. I spotted her higher up the valley, a small figure in the distance heading up towards the loch. A cold wind was blowing through the trees. Rain was coming, I could feel it. I pushed off and followed Rob and Euan down the steep track alongside the river, but all the time I couldn't help thinking we should wait for her.

Euan and Rob were waiting for me by the old quarry.

Euan held open the gate to the mineral track that led down to the village in the valley below. 'You coming with us?' he said.

I shook my head. 'I'll go home across the fields from here. It's quicker.'

I watched them disappear down the mineral track towards the dull orange glow of streetlights in the distance. Daylight was fading fast. It would be dark soon.

Rain started to fall, cold and sharp, like needles of ice. I looked back hoping to see Iona, but I couldn't see her anywhere. She had no coat or shoes, and her clothes were soaked from the river. She would freeze if she stayed up here. People died in these mountains every year, caught out by the weather, unprepared.

I turned my bike and headed back the way I'd come to look for her. Streams of water ran through the deep ruts. I picked up Iona's coat and trainers on the way and stopped at the top of the track to get my breath back. The steep wooded shores of the loch were hidden by the rain. Iona could be anywhere.

I followed the path around to the far side of the loch, calling her name. The clouds were low and heavy. Dark waves slapped against the rocks.

'Iona,' I shouted, but my voice was carried off by the wind.

Maybe I had passed her. Maybe she was already on her way back to the village. I couldn't stay up here all night.

I turned my bike round to head home but my tyre

side-slipped on a rock. I glanced down to see a bare footprint in the mud beside it. Rain had already puddled in the heel and toes.

Iona had come this way.

I jumped off my bike and followed the footprints. It wasn't far along the track before they disappeared. I guessed Iona had left the path and entered the woodland. Moss and pine needles covered the floor.

'Iona,' I called. 'I've got your coat.'

I walked further into the wood. It was dark under the cover of trees, almost too dark to see. I knew Mum and Dad would be wondering where I was.

'Iona,' I called again. But there was no answer.

I turned to go back to my bike, and jumped. Iona stood right in front of me. She had an oversize jumper on, jogging bottoms and a woolly hat that came down over her ears. But her feet were still bare and she shivered with cold.

'I've got your coat and trainers,' I said. I shoved them in her hands. 'Put them on and go home. It'll be dark soon.' I looked around but couldn't see where she'd got her dry clothes from.

Iona pulled her coat on, sat down on a rock and pushed her feet into her trainers. Her hands were shaking and her fingers were blue. She fumbled uselessly with the laces.

I knelt down and tied them up.

She glared at me as I stood up. 'You can't stop me coming here.'

'You heard Rob,' I said. 'You're not wanted. We know you're here now. We'll find you.'

'I have to come back,' she said. The words slipped out, they were barely a whisper.

I shook my head.

'I wasn't stealing,' she said, her teeth chattering. 'I *didn't* have a rod.'

I reached into my coat pocket. 'Have the fish and go,' I said. I threw it on the ground next to her. It rolled in the dirt, coming to rest at her feet.

Iona looked at me and swirled patterns in the pine needles on the ground with her fingers. Circles, round and round and round. 'If you let me back, I'll tell you the secret,' she said.

I stared at her.

She stood up and faced me. 'It's here, on your farm.'

'I know everything on this farm,' I said.

Iona shook her head. 'You don't. You don't know anything about it. No one does.'

'What makes you so sure?' I said.

She glared at me. 'I just know.'

Sky Hawk

How could she know something about my farm that I didn't? Maybe her grandad knew something. Mr McNair was as old as the hills. He used to farm the land next to ours before he moved into the village. But that was years ago, before I was even born.

'What is it then?' I said.

'If I tell you,' she whispered, 'you mustn't tell anyone about it, not your friends, not anyone.'

We just stood, staring at each other in the half light. Wind rushed through the pine branches above us. Rainwater dripped from the trees and pattered on the forest floor.

'All right,' I said.

'And you'll let me back on your farm?' Iona spat on her palm and held it out.

I pulled off my glove, spat on my hand and shook hers. 'Deal.'

She swept her matted hair away from her eyes. 'Tomorrow morning, then,' she said. 'Meet me here, at the loch.'

She picked up the fish, disappeared through the dark trees, and was gone.

CHAPTER 3

It was dark as I cycled down through the fields to the farmhouse. The rain had eased off but I was soaked through. It was hard going, the tyres sucked and slid through the sticky mud. The lights were on in the kitchen, and I could see Mum talking on the phone. I pushed my bike past the lambing shed and kicked the gate open into the yard.

The lambing shed door flung open outlining Dad's silhouette in the doorway.

'Callum, is that you?'

'Yes, Dad.'

'Where've you been?' he said. 'You should have been back hours ago.'

'My bike chain came off,' I lied. 'I'm sorry.'

Sky Hawk

'Go and tell that to your mum,' said Dad. 'She's phoned up half the village trying to find out where you are. She's sent Graham out looking for you. He's mad about it. He's meant to be going out to see a band tonight. I'd better text him.'

I leaned my bike against the wall, kicked my boots off and slipped into the kitchen. My feet left big wet footprints across the stone floor.

'Look at the state of you,' said Mum. 'I was worried sick. You were meant to be back before dark. Rob and Euan said that you've all been up on the river. Graham's up there now, looking for you.'

'Dad's texted him,' I said.

'Go and get changed into some dry clothes and have your tea,' said Mum. 'I'd avoid Graham, if I were you.'

I climbed the stairs to my room and pulled off my wet clothes. My fingers were uselessly cold. I put on a jumper and a fleece, my lined combats and two pairs of socks, but I was still freezing. I thought of Iona. Wherever she was staying, I hoped she'd got there by now. What if she hadn't? I knew where her grandad lived at the edge of the village, but he was Mad Old McNair. I wasn't going there.

I went back down to the kitchen and sat at the table. Dad was there too, tucking into meat pie and chips.

The door slammed and Graham walked past. He didn't even look at me.

Mum passed me a plate of food. I was starving.

Boots clumped on the path outside, and there was a loud knock on the door.

'Come in, Flint,' Mum called.

Flint, Rob's older cousin, came through the door in his bike leathers, helmet in hand. Friday night. He and Graham were going to see a band in the next town.

'Graham won't be long,' said Mum. 'You'll have some pie, won't you, Flint?'

Flint grinned. 'I'd never turn down a piece of your pie, Mrs McGregor. You know me.'

He sat down at the table and leaned into me and whispered, 'I hear you're in the dog-house, little man.'

I forked another chip.

'If it's any comfort,' Flint went on, so Mum and Dad could hear, 'Auntie Sal gave Rob an earful when he got home. He was soaking wet, looked like a drowned rat. He went to bed without any supper.'

I finished my pie. Had Rob told his mum about Iona? I guessed not.

I tried to change the subject. 'Our family's farmed this land for over a hundred years, hasn't it?' I said.

Sky Hawk

Dad looked up. 'About that,' he said. 'Why?'

'Are there any secrets here?'

'Secrets?' said Dad. 'What sort of secrets?'

At that moment Graham walked into the room. He'd showered and changed into his bike leathers. He smelled of shampoo and aftershave. 'There's only one secret I know,' he said, looking right at me. 'It's the shallow grave I'll shove you in, if you *ever* make me late again.'

'Graham!' said Mum. But Graham was already on the way out through the door.

'Thanks, Mrs McGregor,' said Flint following Graham out into the yard.

Their motorbikes roared into life and I watched as the headlights zigzagged down the farm track.

'I can't think of any secrets,' said Dad. 'Why d'you ask?'

I shrugged my shoulders. 'It doesn't matter,' I said. But deep inside I couldn't help feel that there was something none of us knew about, a secret hidden somewhere in the hills and valleys of our farm.

And tomorrow, I was going to find out.

CHAPTER 4

I sat down at breakfast the next morning with my thick fleece jacket and my rucksack by my side.

'Where d'you think you're going?' said Mum.

'Out,' I said.

She raised her eyebrows. 'I don't think so. Not after last night.'

'But Mum . . .'

'We're going to town this morning,' said Mum pouring some tea. 'Dad's got sheep feed to pick up and I've got shopping to do.'

'   ' I said. 'Graham's here.'

'   'You'll come with us.'

'   'It's not fair.'

'   and sighed.

Sky Hawk

'I need someone to look after those two lambs. The foster ewe wasn't interested in them last night. We'll need to bottle feed them until we can find another ewe.'

'I'll do it,' I said. 'I don't want to go to town.'

Mum glared at Dad then turned to me. 'Ah, you'd only get under my feet. You can stay as long as you promise to stay near the farmhouse.'

'I promise,' I said. But underneath the table, my fingers were crossed.

I stood at the sink and stirred milk powder for the lambs into a jug of warm water and watched Mum and Dad drive away down the lane. I poured the milk into two clean bottles and tucked them under my jacket, grabbed my rucksack and headed out to the lambing shed. The two lambs were already bleating hungrily for milk when I went in, and it wasn't long before they finished the milk and started trying to suck on the tags of my coat. I heard the tractor rev into the yard outside. If Graham saw me, I'd have to help him all day. So I left the bottles in a bucket by the door and slipped out through some broken panels at the back of the shed.

The air was clear and sharp. It had rained heavily overnight and the puddles shone in the bright sunlight.

I set off over the back of the hill to the loch in the next valley.

Iona was waiting for me.

'You came then,' she said.

We were standing at the spot where I'd followed her footprints into the wood.

I nodded. 'So what's the secret?'

'You'll find out,' said Iona.

'It'd better be good,' I said.

She turned and headed into the wood.

The pines gave way to oak and birch and wild cherry. I thought I knew every inch of this farm. I'd grown up here. I'd built dens with Rob and Euan all over it. But this path through the trees looked different.

Iona stopped at the edge of a clearing. A ring of large boulders lay in a wide circle in the sunlit space. I leaned against one and pulled some damp moss with my fingers. The pale stone underneath was bright in the spring sunshine. I could imagine this was once a meeting place for the ancient Scottish Warrior Kings.

Iona put her finger to her lips for me to be quiet. 'Fairy stones,' she whispered.

'Fairy stones!' I said. 'You've brought me all this way just to see fairy stones?'

Sky Hawk

Iona giggled. 'Shh! Don't you believe in fairies, Callum?'

I scowled at her. 'I'm going home.'

Iona leaned against the trunk of a tree. It looked as if she was trying not to laugh. She tapped her fingers on the bark. 'Can you climb?' she asked.

I looked up into the tree. It was an old oak that had been struck by lightning some years before. The split trunk looked like a jagged scar against the sky. The nearest branches were beyond arms' reach and the bark was damp and fringed with moss.

'Climb that?' I snapped. 'Course I can.'

Iona kicked off her trainers and slid her fingers and toes into the tiny cracks in the bark. In no time, she had pulled herself up into the fork of branches above.

'Well, are you coming?'

I tried to grip the tree trunk, tried to wedge my feet onto the small ridges of bark, but each time my feet and hands slid. I looked up, but Iona had disappeared further up the tree.

'Iona!' I called. The end of a thick knotted rope fell by my feet. I hauled myself up into the tree and climbed higher to a natural platform of spreading branches. It was like a hidden fortress. You couldn't see it from the ground. Iona had made seats from old crates and there were tins and boxes and an old hurricane lamp balanced in the tree. From there, I could see across the narrow waters of the loch to the mountains and the wide blue sky beyond.

'It's brilliant,' I said, 'brilliant.'

'Shh, you've got to be quiet,' she said. She pulled a canvas bag out from the hollow trunk and spilled out a blanket, an old leather case, and a packet of biscuits.

'I promise I won't tell anyone about this,' I whispered.

She threw me a biscuit and stifled a laugh. 'This isn't the secret, dummy. It's better than this, a million times better.'

I stuffed the biscuit in my mouth. 'What is it then?'

She pointed to a cluster of Scots pine-trees on the island not far from the shore. The tall bare trunks were crowned by a spread of branches, dense with green pine needles. From our platform of crates, we were level with the flattened tree tops.

'What's so special?' I said.

'Open your eyes, Callum,' said Iona. 'Look!'

I still couldn't see what she was pointing at. A pile of sticks lay on the topmost branches, like driftwood stacked on a high tide.

But something was moving inside. Something was pulling the sticks into place. It wasn't just a random heap of twigs and branches. Something was building it.

And then I saw it.

Sky Hawk

I saw the secret hidden in our valley. No one else knew about it. Not Mum or Dad, or Graham, or Rob and Euan.

Just me, and Iona.

'Amazing isn't it?' whispered Iona.

I just nodded.

I was lost for words.

CHAPTER 5

At first all I could see was the head of a bird above the pile of sticks, a creamy head with a brown stripe across the eye. Then the rest of the bird appeared. It was huge, with dark brown wings and a white belly. There was something prehistoric about it, like a beast of a lost world, too big for this landscape.

'Osprey,' I whispered. I could hardly believe it. 'We've got osprey, here, on our farm.'

'You won't tell a soul?' said Iona.

'Course not,' I said. I'd seen photos of ospreys before, and I'd seen the nesting tree of two ospreys at the nearby nature reserve when I'd helped Dad put up fencing and bird hides. The nesting tree at the reserve had razor wire and surveillance cameras to stop people stealing the eggs.

Sky Hawk

'They're rare, they are,' I said. 'They're protected.'

'I knew I could trust you,' said Iona. She emptied out the biscuit packet. There was only one left. She broke it in two and gave me the bigger half.

'I've watched him build that nest from scratch,' said Iona.

'What makes you think it's a "he"?' I said.

Iona pulled out a bird book from the leather case and showed me the picture. 'Female ones have got more brown markings on the chest,' she said. 'And he keeps circling up high in the sky and calling. He's looking for a mate. I've been watching him all week.'

'Do you live up here then?' I said.

Iona laughed and shook her head. 'No, I'd like to, though. I'm staying with my grandad, for now.'

'What about your ma?' I said. 'Is she here too?'

Iona frowned. 'Ma's working.' She picked pine needles from her jumper and flicked them in the air. 'She's a dancer, you know,' said Iona. 'My ma, she's a dancer.' She pulled out a small gold locket on a chain from under her shirt and opened it. 'That's her.'

On one side was a picture of Iona and on the other, a picture of a young woman's face. She had flaming red hair and dark eyes like Iona's.

'She's in all the big shows in London,' said Iona. 'She's

too busy to come up here. She's really famous, my ma.'

'I've never heard of her,' I said.

Iona scowled and stuffed the locket back under her shirt. 'As if you'd know!'

I looked across at the osprey again. He was standing on the nest staring up at the sky. His high-pitched cry called out, 'Kee . . . kee . . . kee . . . '

'Has he finished his nest?' I said.

'Don't think so,' said Iona. 'It keeps getting bigger and bigger. Anyway, it's called an *eyrie*, not a nest. Ospreys go to Africa in the winter.'

'I know that,' I said. 'You're not the only one who knows this stuff.'

The osprey marched around his eyrie and called out one more time. Then he spread his huge wings and lifted off into the air. He banked away over the trees behind us, showing the brown striped underside of his wings and his white belly.

'He's probably gone fishing,' said Iona. 'Might be ages before he's back.'

'I've got to go,' I said. I remembered the orphan lambs. They'd need another feed soon.

'I'm going back too,' said Iona.

I helped her stuff the bag into the hollow of the tree and

dropped down to the ground beside her. We walked along the track by the river. The air was warm now, and wisps of steam rose up from the damp earth.

'How was the fish?' I asked.

Iona gave me a wicked grin. 'Delicious.'

'How d'you do it?' I said. 'How d'you catch it with your bare hands?'

Iona grinned.

'Come on, I'll show you.'

I followed her to the river's edge where eddies of fast-water swirled into a still pool. 'What do you see?' she said.

I lay down on the soft grass and looked at the river water. Cloud and sunlight reflected back. 'Nothing,' I said.

'You're not doing it right,' said Iona. 'Look further in.'

I stared at the water. Cloud patterns floated across it. I tried to look beyond the bright surface to the dark shadows below. The rocks merged into the brownish river bed. It was all moving and shifting. Reed, mud, and silt-stirred leaves. And two fish. Two trout, facing the current, their green-speckled bodies perfectly still except for the ripple of their tails.

'D'you see them?' whispered Iona.

I nodded.

'Now run your hand slowly into the water behind them.'

I slid my hand into the river. Closer and closer until my fingers were inches from their tails.

'Run your fingers underneath and try to stroke behind their gills,' said Iona.

I reached forward, and for a moment felt the slippery body of one fish against my hand before both fish shot into the deep water and were gone.

Iona laughed. 'It took me ages at first,' she said. 'Grandad showed me one summer when I was little.'

I stared deep into the water, hoping to see the fish return.

'People are like rivers,' said Iona. 'That's what I think.'

I sat up and squeezed the water from my sleeve. 'What d'you mean?'

Iona rocked back on her heels and looked right at me. 'You've got to learn to look beneath the surface, to see what lies deeper in.'

I stuffed my hands in my pockets. They were freezing from the icy water. 'I've got to go now.'

'So can I come back?' said Iona. 'On your farm?'

I nodded. 'We made a deal, didn't we?'

Iona stood up and smiled. 'A female osprey will come tomorrow afternoon,' she said. 'There's good weather coming. She'll be here, I'm sure of it.'

I laughed. 'Oh, right. You just know, do you?'

Sky Hawk

Iona turned her back on me. 'Meet me up on the hill tomorrow if you don't believe me. I'm going to wait for her.'

I looked up at the heather-covered hill above us. I could see the silhouette of the cairn on top, the highest point of the farm. It would be perfect. I wanted to see an osprey coming back to Scotland. I wanted to see it with my own eyes. It would be amazing to have ospreys nesting here, on our farm.

'All right, Iona,' I said. 'You're on.'

CHAPTER 6

'You did a good job with those lambs yesterday,' said Dad. 'Maybe we'll make a farmer of you yet.'

I sat in the back of the car behind Mum and Dad on the way to church.

'Do I have to go to church?' I said. 'Graham doesn't.'

'He's eighteen,' Mum said. 'It's up to him.'

'Rob doesn't go, or Euan.'

Mum spun round to look at me. 'For goodness' sake, Callum, will you stop your whinging. It's only an hour. It's not going to kill you.'

I could see the corner of Dad's eyes crinkle in the mirror. He was laughing at me. I slumped down and shoved my knees in the back of his seat.

'Have you got any plans today?' said Dad.

Sky Hawk

'Playing football,' I said, 'with Rob and Euan and others from school.' It was true; we said we'd meet on Sunday afternoon and kick a ball about in the playing field. But I kept thinking of Iona, and watching an osprey return. I wanted to go back up to the loch. I'd have to tell Rob and Euan I was helping Dad on the farm instead.

'Just make sure you're back for tea,' said Mum.

Iona was already standing on the cairn when I reached the top of the hill. I flopped down in the heather to get my breath back. The sky was cloudless. The loch was flat, like a mirror, reflecting the blue, blue sky. I focused my binoculars on the eyrie in the pine tree. The osprey was pulling more sticks into place.

'Here,' I said. 'D'you want a look?'

Iona put the binoculars to her eyes, and I showed her how to focus them. 'It's brilliant,' she said. 'He looks so close. And look at his beak. It's vicious, that beak. Look how sharp it is.'

I let Iona use the binoculars and I looked south. Aeroplane trails criss-crossed the sky and a flock of geese flew in a V-shape in the far distance, but otherwise, the horizon was empty. I leaned back into the soft heather, out of the cold tug of wind. The sun was warm on my face, and I felt my eyelids close.

I woke feeling chilled and cold. Iona was still sitting on the cairn looking at the sky. Shadows had crept across the glen below, and I looked at my watch.

'We've been up here two hours now,' I said to Iona. 'There's no osprey coming.'

She gave me a hard stare.

'She'll be here soon enough.'

I stripped the end of a sprig of heather and watched the small pieces scatter in the breeze. I flicked the bare stem at her.

'I knew I should've played football instead.'

Iona turned her back on me. 'You didn't have to come.'

'I'm missing a good game,' I said.

'She'll come from over there,' said Iona. She pointed across the bright waters of the loch to the heather hills and the smudge of purple mountains beyond.

'How d'you *know*?' I said.

She stood up and stretched her arms wide like outspread wings. 'I just know. I can feel it. You have to imagine you're a bird, to feel it.'

'I'm not flapping my arms and running about the hills, if that's what you think.'

Sky Hawk

Iona shrugged her shoulders. The wind lifted the tangled ends of her hair.

'Flap around all you like,' I said. 'I'm off.' I shook the bits of heather from my jumper and set off down the hill kicking hummocks of dry grass. I turned to look at her but she just stood, arms wide, her eyes closed. The wind rippled across her coat and jeans. It looked as if she was soaring against the clear blue sky.

'You really think she's coming?' I said.

'I know so. You should really try this, Callum.'

I scowled at her.

'No one can see you up here,' she said lifting her arms higher.

'Just as well then,' I said. I stretched my arms and turned to face the wind. I wanted to believe Iona. I wanted to see an osprey come back.

'You've got to close your eyes,' Iona called. 'Become bird. Feel for the wind, Callum. Let it carry you.'

I closed my eyes and tried to forget I was standing on a hillside like some stupid scarecrow. All I could hear was the soft hiss of wind rushing through the dry heather. It flowed over me, tugging at the sleeves of my jumper. I leaned into it, letting it run through the tips of my fingers. I stretched them wide, like feathers. I tried to imagine I was a bird, weightless, carried up, up, up into the bright blue sky. Up, above the mountains. Up, into the fast winds. Up, up, up into the splintered rays of sun.

'I can see her,' cried Iona.

I opened my eyes and squinted into the sunlight. There was a silhouette of a bird in the distance, like the shape small children draw seagulls. But it wasn't a seagull. It was bigger than that, much bigger.

The bird flew closer and banked in the air, showing the white of its belly and barred wing and tail feathers. I looked through the binoculars.

'It's definitely an osprey,' I said.

'Of course it is,' said Iona. 'Come on, let's get a closer look.'

We ran down the hillside towards the wooded shores of the loch.

Iona was already darting through the trees ahead of me. When I pulled myself up into the oak tree, Iona was sitting on the wooden crates, her eyes shining. 'Look, he's spotted her,' she said.

I looked across at the eyrie. The male was perched on the top, his wings held slightly open showing the white underneath. He suddenly lifted up into the sky carrying a fish. Up he flew, higher and higher. We could hear his high pitched cry, 'Kee . . . kee . . . kee.' Then he swooped and dived, plummeting downwards, the fish held in his talons. He was a blur against the wooded hillside, faster and faster towards the water, until he pulled out of his dive and flew high in the air once more. The female soared in circles above, watching.

'He's sky-dancing,' said Iona with a grin. 'He's trying to impress her.'

The male did his spectacular high dive trick again, but this time pulled up from his dive and flew to the eyrie with the fish.

We watched the female circle lower and lower until she landed on a tree next to him. She clung on to a branch as it swayed beneath her, inspecting the eyrie. I held my breath.

But she suddenly flapped her wings and flew off over the trees behind us and was gone.

'She's not impressed,' I said.

I focused my binoculars on the male osprey. I almost laughed. If a bird could look totally let down, he did then. The feathers on his head were all ruffled and he kept looking at his fish as if it was all the fish's fault.

'Here she comes again,' whispered Iona.

The female swooped in, low and wide, and landed right on the eyrie. She paced around the edge and pulled a few sticks into place as though it wasn't quite to her liking. Then she pulled the fish away from the male and started tearing off chunks of flesh.

Iona leaned into me and nudged me. 'Look, she likes him.'

I nodded, and for some reason felt my face burn bright red.

CHAPTER 7

I sprinkled brown sugar onto my porridge and watched it melt into sticky golden pools.

'That'll rot your teeth,' said Dad. He sprinkled salt and a small lump of butter on his own porridge and swirled it round. He looked tired and grumpy. I guessed he'd been up in the night checking the ewes that were due to lamb.

'You were late coming back from football yesterday,' said Dad. He flicked through a farming magazine beside him. 'Graham and I could've done with some help.'

I wanted to tell them I was up on the hills watching an osprey come back. I was bursting to tell them we had ospreys nesting here, on our farm. But it was a secret, Iona's and my secret. We'd promised to tell no one.

Graham poured a cup of tea and laughed. 'He wasn't

playing football yesterday. He was up on the hill flapping round like a wee birdie. I saw him with a girl up there.' He turned to me. 'Your girlfriend, is she?'

I hit him on the arm and tea spilled across the table.

'Och! Grow up, you two, for heaven's sake,' said Mum. 'Graham, you're old enough to know better.' She mopped the tea from the table and sat back in the rocker chair warming her feet on the cooking range. 'Which girl's this?'

Graham raised his eyebrows. 'It looked like Mad Old McNair's granddaughter to me.'

'I heard she was back,' said Mum.

'Fiona McNair's child?' said Dad. He turned to Mum. 'You were at school with Fiona, weren't you?'

Mum nodded. 'Aye, that was a while ago. There's a lot of water gone under the bridge since then.'

'Rob hates the McNairs,' I said. 'He says Iona's mum stole from his dad and ruined his business. Is it true?'

Mum started clearing the table. 'It's true that a lot of money went missing the day Fiona left,' she sighed. 'But truth be told, Rob's dad was never much of a businessman anyway.'

'He was trying to build an adventure park,' said Dad, 'bike trails through the forest, and high wire stuff in the trees. It was losing money before Fiona worked there.'

Sky Hawk

'She's a dancer, isn't she?' I said. 'That's what Iona says. She's in the big shows down in London.'

Mum and Dad exchanged glances and Dad went back to reading his magazine. 'Well, I haven't heard from her for a while,' said Mum. 'But I heard she did a bit of dancing.'

Graham gave a snort of laughter.

Dad glared at him. 'Haven't you got sheep to feed?'

Graham reached for his coat and gave me a slap on the back. 'Off to school now,' he grinned. 'Don't be late.'

It wasn't fair. Graham was eighteen. He'd finished school and was back on the farm where he'd always wanted to be. Mum and Dad even let him live in the cottage up the track which had been Granda's before he died. Graham said he needed his own space. I didn't think Mum should cook his meals and wash all his clothes too.

'What's she like?' asked Mum.

'Who, Iona?' I said. I shrugged my shoulders. 'How should I know?'

I whizzed into school as the bell rang. It was Monday morning and I was late. I pushed my bike into the rack next to Rob's and raced to the classroom. The rest of the class were already in their seats. The teacher gave me a hard stare and tapped her watch as I sat down next to Rob and Euan.

'What happened to you on Friday?' whispered Euan. 'You didn't get home for hours after we left you. Mum made me tell her where we'd been.'

It seemed ages ago, although it was only three days.

'I was checking on sheep,' I lied.

'You'll never guess who's in our class,' said Rob. His face was dark, like thunder. He nodded to the tables at the front of the class. 'It's her.'

At that moment Iona turned round. It was as if she could feel us looking at her. She looked strangely out of place in the classroom, in her grey uniform and blue fleece. Her hair was tied in a ponytail, but thick clumps and tangles stuck out at the back. She smiled at me, but I looked away.

'Nutter,' said Rob.

Our teacher introduced Iona, but most of the class knew of her. At least they knew her grandad, and that was enough to set some of the girls off giggling.

At lunch-break I saw Iona alone. She sat on the far wall of the playground staring out over the fields. I joined a group from my class trading cards.

'She forgot her lunch,' said Ruth. 'She won't tell the teachers though.'

'Look at the state of her,' said Sarah. 'I don't see why *she*

Sky Hawk

should be allowed to wear trainers when no one else can.'

Ruth spread her cards out on the table. 'I heard her ma's locked up in a mental home.'

Sarah picked a card and swapped it for one of hers. 'Mum said to have nothing to do with her.'

'Why?' I asked.

'Cos she's a nutter,' said Rob. 'You've seen that yourself.'

I saved a sandwich for Iona, but didn't get a chance to give it to her until afternoon class. The teacher let Iona pick someone to work with in the library for our class project on recycling, and she picked me.

'Thanks,' said Iona. She wolfed the sandwich down and wiped the crumbs from her chin.

We sat in the corner of the library and spread out books in front of us.

No one else was in there. The sun poured through the big side windows.

'Look at this book,' said Iona.

She sat down next to me and opened a large book on Scottish wildlife and started flicking through the pages. 'You've got a pine-marten den on your farm, did you know?'

I leaned across to look at the picture of the creature sitting in the branch of a tree. Its long brown body looked part-cat, part-weasel. I'd only caught a glimpse of a pine-marten once before, just its face peering above an old fallen trunk. It had turned and disappeared into the undergrowth showing a last view of its bushy tail. I flicked over to another page. Iona seemed to know more about my farm than I did.

'I've seen golden eagles before,' I said.

'Really?' said Iona. 'I've never seen one of them.'

'Last year, I saw them. On the other side of the hill,' I said. 'We'll look for them.'

Iona smiled. 'I'd like that.'

I leaned across Iona to point to a photo of red deer, 'And we've got those . . . '

'Callum!'

I jumped. I hadn't heard the library door open. Rob was standing behind us, staring at me. I leapt to my feet.

'Time to pack up,' said Rob. He scowled at Iona.

Iona went back to flicking through her book.

I ignored her and started putting books away on the shelves.

'Come on,' said Rob, 'it's home time. Let her do the rest.'

I followed Rob out through the door and into the playground. We pulled our bikes from the rack and pushed them out past the mums and dads waiting at the school gates. Mad Old McNair was standing on the other side of the road, a stooped figure in a long brown coat. As we cycled past, I noticed striped pyjamas flap against his bare legs.

'Race you,' said Rob.

I pedalled like mad behind Rob up the hill out of the village. When we got to the top of the hill, I glanced back down the road. The village lay sprawled out like a map beneath us, the bright green of the playing field dotted with a few sheep, the village hall and the shop and the stone cottages.

The school playground had emptied, and cars were winding their way along the narrow roads. A stooped figure shuffled slowly along the south road out of the village. A smaller figure behind him turned to look up and waved.

'Come on,' said Rob. 'What are you waiting for?'

I didn't wave back.

Instead, I turned my bike down the steep descent of Shepherd's Lane, my wheels following in Rob's tyre tracks all the way.

CHAPTER 8

The next morning Rob was waiting for me at the bottom of our farm track with a great fat grin on his face. 'Well, what d'you reckon?' he said.

I looked at his new mountain bike, shining black and silver.

'Jammy,' I said. 'I forgot it was your birthday today.'

'I couldn't believe Dad got me this one,' Rob said. 'It's a top model. Front and rear disc brakes, Shimano gears, front suspension forks, it's got the lot. And look at this.' He pointed to a small oval panel clipped to the frame. 'It's a bike computer. My auntie got it for me. It tells my speed, altitude, distance travelled . . . it does everything.'

I pushed off on my own bike. 'Bet it doesn't make you faster,' I yelled.

Sky Hawk

I raced away. I loved mornings like this, bright sunlight on the potholed puddles. We were fairly level on the flat, but Rob pulled away from me in Shepherd's Lane, up through the rough tracks. My tyres couldn't grip the loose stones, and I had to get off and push my bike the rest of the way.

Rob was wiping the mud off his alloy wheels and talking to Euan when I reached the bike shed. Iona was hovering nearby, but I pretended I hadn't seen her.

'Are you coming round tonight?' Rob asked us. 'Mum's cooking pizzas.'

'I've got a cool new DVD I'll bring,' said Euan.

Rob rolled his eyes. 'Let me guess, "A Hundred Places to go Fly-Fishing Before You Die".'

'It's "Extreme Fishing", actually,' said Euan. 'It's got sharks and barracudas.'

'Save it for another day,' said Rob. 'I can't take the excitement.'

I shouldered my bag and walked with Rob and Euan across the wet playground to the far wall. Rob took out his homework and copied some of Euan's answers, scrawling them down on his worksheets. Iona was leaning against the wall not far from us, watching me. The bell rang and children started to move towards their classrooms.

'Come on,' said Euan, 'we've got class.'

Rob stuffed his homework in his bag and we hurried up the ramp to the classroom. I was at the door when Iona called me back.

'What does she want?' Rob frowned.

I shrugged my shoulders. 'I'll catch you up.' I turned to Iona.

'You coming to the loch after school?' she asked.

'I can't,' I said. 'It's Rob's birthday.'

'Doesn't matter.' She smiled and passed me a large envelope. 'I did this for you last night.'

I could see Rob watching us from the window.

'Thanks, Iona,' I mumbled. I stuffed it in my bag.

'Aren't you going to look inside?' she said.

'Later,' I said. 'Come on, we're late.'

I walked to the back of the room and slung my bag on the table with Rob and Euan. The teacher wasn't in the class yet, so I took my homework out of my bag and walked up through the aisle between the tables to place it on the teacher's desk.

When I got back to my chair, Euan and Rob were crowded over my bag. They'd pulled out the envelope and opened it and were looking at a painting on a piece of paper.

'Very romantic,' said Euan with a grin.

I looked at the paper. Iona had painted two ospreys. One was sitting in the nest and the other was flying, wings outspread, bringing a fish. She had signed it: 'To Callum, from Iona. xxx.'

'She's always watching you,' said Rob. 'I reckon she fancies you!'

'Does not,' I mumbled.

'Look at all these kisses,' said Rob.

I wished he'd just shut up. Iona was looking at us now.

'Her grandad came down to the shop in his night-shirt last week,' said Euan. 'Night-shirt and slippers, that's all he had on.'

Rob looked across my shoulder to where Iona was sitting.

'Right nutters, the pair of them,' he said. 'Should be banged up in a mental home.' He held up the picture in full view. The rest of the class was listening now. Some of the girls laughed. Rob's voice was crystal sharp, loud and clear. 'Right nutters. What d'you reckon, Callum?'

I could see Iona watching me from under her fringe of red hair. I could feel her eyes burning into me.

The whole class was watching.

I looked down at my shoes, where mud had hardened into a thick brown shell. 'Yeah, right pair of nutters,' I said.

CHAPTER 9

I pushed the front wheel of my bike out to the edge. The earth crumbled beneath the tyre sending small stones skittering down the steep gulley. In winter, it had been a torrent of water from the hills but now it was a vertical drop of mud and stone.

'Death Drop,' Rob grinned. 'Wipe-Out Alley.' He pushed the buttons on the tiny panel of his bike computer. 'It'll record it all,' he said, 'gradient, speed, cadence . . . everything.'

I gripped my handlebars, blood pumping in my ears.

'Ready?' Rob's face lit up with his maniac smile.

I nodded.

Rob fiddled with the camera fixed to his helmet. 'I'll come after you on my bike. Don't knock me off. I nicked this action-cam from my dad. He doesn't know I've got it.'

I stared into the abyss below me. If all went OK I'd level out on the flat and shoot up the bank the far side.

'OK,' said Rob. 'Five . . . '

Why am I doing this?

'Four . . . '

I'm going to die.

'Three . . . '

I can't . . .

'Two . . . '

I CAN'T!

'One . . . '

Do it.

'Go . . . '

The ground was gone.

I was flying . . . falling. Down, down, down. Lean back, lean back, my mind screamed. I hit ground, grit and stone spraying from my back wheel where it jammed and jarred into the deep running grooves of the gulley, twisting metal spokes as my front wheel slammed onto a hummock of grass and lurched me forward, flying through the air. Over and over and over, tumbling in a whirl of legs, arms, and bike, plummeting downwards past a blur of mud and stones and heather, over and over and over, all the way down the

CHAPTER 9

waterfall gulley to the rutted track below. I landed upside-down in a heap of heather to see Rob fly up over the bank, perform a perfect half spin in the air and disappear the other side.

There was silence followed by a loud splash.

'Watch what you're bloody doing,' shouted Euan's voice.

'You were in the way,' Rob yelled back.

I lay there listening to them argue. I moved my legs and arms. It didn't feel as if I had any broken bones and it didn't look as though Rob or Euan were going to come and find out either. I hobbled up the bank to see Rob and Euan sprawling in the shallows of the river.

Euan gave Rob's bike a kick. 'You could've broke my rod, you bloody idiot.'

Rob picked his bike up and dragged it to the bank, laughing. 'Good one, Callum! I got it all on camera.'

'An' you've scared off all the fish,' shouted Euan. 'I won't catch anything with you mucking about.'

'Sure you're using the right fly?' shouted Rob, pulling some chocolate from his bag.

Euan turned to glare at him. 'As if you'd know,' he said.

I pushed my bike over to Rob.

'Guess how long till he tells us he's the fly fishing champion,' I grinned.

Sky Hawk

'I heard that,' shouted Euan. 'I didn't get the junior fly fishing cup for nothing, you know!'

'Catch . . . ' yelled Rob and he threw Euan a chocolate bar. ' . . . it might be the only thing you do catch today.'

'Ta,' Euan muttered. 'You just wait, Rob,' he said. 'Fly fishing is pure skill, none of your computer techno stuff. You just wait.'

I sat down in the soft grass and rubbed my bruised legs. Rob passed me some chocolate and we watched the playback on the action-cam. I thought I'd been in control for some of the death drop, but all I could see was me tumbling over and over.

Rob laughed. 'It's mind over matter. You and the bike, you *are* the bike.'

I looked at my bike, at the deep scratches in the paintwork and bent wheel spokes. 'I know what you mean,' I groaned.

The sun was so hot, more like a summer's day than one in May. The rest of the half term holiday stretched ahead of us. I lay back, closed my eyes and let the chocolate slowly melt in my mouth.

It was over a month ago I'd sat with Iona on the heather hillside and seen the osprey return. I hadn't seen much of Iona since then. I think she was avoiding me. I wanted to say sorry about the mean things I'd said about her and her grandad, but there was never a good time. I often went to the loch to watch the ospreys. I'd even seen the male osprey catch a fish in his talons right out of the loch, but it just wasn't the same without Iona to share it with.

'I'VE GOT ONE,' shouted Euan.

Rob and I scrambled down the bank.

Euan was thigh deep in water, his rod arched downstream. 'Here it comes,' he said. The end of the rod bowed and bent against the fighting strain of the fish. A silvery underbelly flashed as the fish leapt from the water's surface, twisting in the air before plunging back under water.

'I've got you, I've got you!' Euan reeled the fish onto the stony bank. 'Rainbow trout,' said Euan with a grin. 'Not a bad size.'

We watched the fish gulp and thrash on the ground at our feet. Its smooth scales glittered a million colours in the bright sunshine. The scarlet gills desperately flapped the air. I wanted to pick it up and let it slide back into the cool river water. I wanted to watch it skim away under the bright surface. But Euan hit it over the head with a stick.

'CALLUM!'

We'd been so engrossed looking at the fish that we hadn't seen Iona on the bank above us. Her face was red from running.

Sky Hawk

'Callum, you've got to come!' she shouted.

Rob and Euan were looking at me.

I wanted to call Iona over to join us. I wanted them to like her.

'I thought you'd got rid of her,' said Rob.

'Can't it wait?' I called to Iona.

Iona slid down the bank and pulled me away from the others. I could see now she had been crying, tears streaked against her face.

'It's the osprey,' she whispered. Her voice was thick and choked. 'I think she's dead.'

CHAPTER 10

'Come *on*, Callum,' said Iona tugging at my sleeve.
Rob and Euan were staring at me.

I turned back to Iona. 'Where is she?' I said.

'Back at the loch.'

'Hey, Callum,' yelled Rob. 'Let's go and ride the top trail.'

'We've got to hurry,' said Iona.

Rob was walking over to us now.

'Look, Iona . . . ' I said, 'I can't . . . '

'Fine!' spat Iona. 'Don't bother. Stay with your mates.'

She picked up my bike, swung her leg over and pushed off down the track.

'Iona!' I shouted. But she was already racing towards the road over the stone bridge. I looked at Rob's bike by my feet. It was his pride and joy, the Formula One model of all mountain bikes. I pulled it up, moulding my hands round the handlebars.

'Oi, Callum!' Rob yelled. 'Leave my bike alone.'

I glanced at him over my shoulder.

'Not my bike,' Rob yelled. 'Not my bike.'

I pushed off, slipping smoothly through the gears. The frame absorbed the stones and ruts, and the tyres gripped the thick mud. I flew down the track after Iona.

'I'll kill you, Callum. I'll bloody kill you.' But Rob's voice was soon drowned in the rush of river under the bridge.

I caught up with Iona at the bottom of the mineral track. We cycled up past the old quarries following the riverbank. My legs ached and my lungs burned.

'Come on,' said Iona.

I pushed Rob's bike up to the top of the track.

'There,' Iona shouted, when we reached the edge of the loch.

I looked across the dark waters to the island.

My mouth went dry.

I felt sick.

Hanging below one of the branches of the nest tree was the osprey, slowly turning as if held by invisible thread. She spun in mid-air, upside-down, like a gruesome ballet dancer. Feet skyward, wings pointing to the ground.

'Fishing line,' said Iona. 'I reckon she's tangled in fishing line.'

There was no movement from the osprey. Her body hung slack and limp. I clapped my hands, once, twice. It echoed across the loch.

The osprey jerked upwards. Her wings uselessly beat the air, and she swung like a pendulum beneath her eyrie, backwards and forwards, backwards and forwards.

Her alarm cry rang out, 'Kee . . . kee . . . kee . . . '

'She'll die,' said Iona. 'She'll die like that.'

I looked at the tree. 'We can't climb that. It's way too high,' I said. 'It must be over a hundred feet tall.'

'You've got some ropes on the farm,' said Iona.

I looked at her. Her face was set.

'You need the proper tree climbing stuff,' I said. 'Harnesses and abseil ropes and things.'

Iona put her hands on her hips. 'We can't just let her die.'

'I know,' I said. I squinted into the sun. The osprey was still again. 'We'll have to get help.'

'And tell someone our secret?' said Iona. She was furious. 'Never.'

'We've got no choice,' I said.

'You promised, Callum,' she said. 'If you don't go up there, I will.'

Sky Hawk

I kicked the ground. 'And what if we do get her down? She's bound to be injured. What then? You'll know what to do, will you?'

Iona pressed her palms into her eyes. 'We can't let her die,' she sobbed.

'Come on,' I said. I picked Rob's bike up and pushed off down the track. 'We can't do this on our own.'

CHAPTER 11

Dad hung up the telephone receiver on the kitchen wall. 'That was Hamish from the nature reserve,' he said. 'He's coming to help.'

'He mustn't tell anyone about the ospreys,' said Iona.

'You don't have to worry,' said Dad. 'He's in charge of the ospreys at the reserve. He'll keep quiet about it.'

'He better had,' said Iona, pacing up and down.

Dad smiled and whistled softly under his breath. 'Who'd have thought, eh? We've got ospreys here, on our farm.'

An hour later we were in the back of the Land Rover bumping along the top field.

'Hold on tight back there!' yelled Dad as the Land Rover bucked over the hummocks of grass.

Sky Hawk

Hamish didn't look much older than some of my cousins. I guessed he was twenty-three, maybe twenty-four. He came with a big grin and a whole load of stuff: harnesses and ropes to climb the tree, scales to weigh the osprey, and a kit to put a ring on her leg. He crammed them all around us and sat on a bag of ropes, holding a small black case carefully on his lap.

I liked him straight away and I could tell he liked us too. As the Land Rover lurched over the rough ground, Iona told Hamish about the pine-martens' den she'd found in a hollowed tree and about the golden plovers that nested on the moorlands and the herd of red deer that grazed the high slopes above the farm. And Hamish listened, I mean really listened.

'You'll be putting me out of work,' Hamish laughed.

The Land Rover slithered and slipped in the muddy track beside the river, and Hamish tightened his grip on the black case.

'What's in there?' asked Iona.

'This?' said Hamish. He tapped the side of the small black case. 'You'll have to wait and see. I only hope we get a chance to use it.'

Dad pulled up at the end of the loch where our small rowing boat lay on the gritty shore.

'Where is she?' said Hamish.

'There,' I said. I pointed across the loch to the island. The osprey hung below the eyrie, like a corpse. She spun slowly, round and round and round.

Iona covered her face in her hands. 'She's dead, isn't she?'

Hamish focused his binoculars on her. 'I can't tell,' he muttered. 'But she's got company.'

A pair of crows tumbled from the sky, and swooped at her from the side. She suddenly lurched up, beat her wings and jabbed at them with her beak, but I could see she was already much weaker.

'Come on,' urged Iona. 'We've not got much time.'

Dad and Hamish rowed. I sat in the prow of the boat and Iona sat holding Hamish's small black case. It took for ever to reach the island, and all the time the crows bombed and dived at the osprey.

'Look!' said Iona. 'The other osprey.'

The osprey's mate appeared at the nest. We could hear his high piercing alarm calls. He chased the crows, twisting and turning in the air, but they flew into the cover of a branch thick with pine needles, where they cawed, mocking him.

The boat crunched on the rocky shore of the island. We

hauled the stuff out of the boat, and Dad helped Hamish into his climbing harness. He fed the rope as Hamish climbed higher and higher up into the tree. The male osprey flew off to the other side of the loch, where he watched us from the top of a tree. Hamish worked his way along one of the branches below the eyrie. The branch bowed and dipped as he edged out towards the osprey. I could hardly watch.

'He's got her,' Dad said.

Hamish sat astride the branch pulling the osprey upwards. Soon he was hidden behind a huge pair of beating wings. We heard Hamish cry out once, before he folded the wings and pushed the osprey into a canvas bag around his waist. He inspected the nest briefly, and then dropped down on the rope, like a puppet on a string, to the ground beside us.

'She's a bit feisty, mind,' said Hamish. He wiped some blood from a fresh cut on the side of his chin. 'Still, it's a good sign, I guess.'

We crouched on the ground next to him. Hamish untied the straps around the sling holding the osprey. She struggled inside and I could hear the scratch of talons on the rough canvas.

'Are you ready for this?' said Hamish. His face was

deadly serious. 'I mean are you *really* ready?'

Iona and I leaned forward. We couldn't take our eyes off the sling holding the osprey.

Hamish pushed his hands into long leather gauntlets, and then slowly and carefully unfurled the canvas.

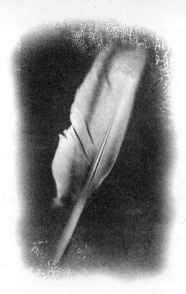

CHAPTER 12

Nothing prepared me for seeing her right in front of me. It was as if the lochs and the mountains and the sky were folded deep inside her, as if she was a small piece of this vast landscape and none of it could exist without her.

'Grab some more gloves, Callum,' Hamish said. 'I'll need a hand here.'

I pulled the thick leather gloves up to my sleeves and wrapped my hands around the osprey's folded wings. I thought she'd be really heavy, but she was light, much lighter than I expected, as if she was made out of air itself. My hands were shaking. I didn't want to hurt her and I didn't want to be on the sharp end of her talons.

'She's got three eggs up there,' said Hamish. 'Take a look while I set this stuff up.'

Iona showed me the picture on Hamish's phone. There were three creamy white eggs with chocolatey brown smudges in a bed of soft grass.

'She's been off the nest a while now,' said Hamish. 'We'd better work fast or the chicks inside might die.'

Hamish weighed the osprey in another sling with weighing scales. 'Good weight,' Hamish nodded. 'Let's check her over.'

He gently spread out each wing. The feathers weren't just plain brown, but all the colours from dark furrowed fields to pale golden wheat. When Hamish stretched them out, her wingspan was as long as me.

'Look at those talons,' said Dad. 'They could do some damage.'

'She's a fish-killing machine all right,' said Hamish. 'See here, her foot has ridges and spiky scales to hold on to slippery fish.'

I had to touch her talons. I took my gloves off and felt the smooth perfect curve of each talon and the needle-sharp tip.

'Careful,' said Hamish. 'Once she's got you, she won't let go.'

'She's beautiful, isn't she?' said Iona.

I nodded. But it was the osprey's eyes that fascinated me.

Sky Hawk

They were sunflower yellow, bright and intense. When she fixed me with her eyes it was as if she was looking right into me, as if I couldn't hide anything from her.

'I reckon we got to her just in time,' said Hamish. 'She's got Iona to thank for that. That fishing line has cut right into her foot.'

I helped to cut the long strands of fishing line. The osprey flinched as Hamish gently pulled them from her foot. The line had cut through the skin and deep into the flesh and we could see shiny whiteness inside.

'She's lucky,' said Hamish. 'That's her tendon in there. If the line had cut the tendon, she wouldn't be able to grasp with her foot. She'd never be able to fish again.'

'Will we need to keep her in for a few days,' asked Dad, 'till it heals?'

Hamish shook his head. 'I'll spray it with some antiseptic. It should heal OK,' he said. 'These birds don't do so well in captivity, and anyway, her mate will feed her while she sits on her eggs.'

'So can we let her go now?' asked Iona.

'Soon,' said Hamish. 'Open that little black case will you, Iona.'

Iona undid the plastic catches and opened the lid. Inside was a small rectangular black box, a long thin wire, and small harness that looked as if it would fit a toy bear.

'It's a satellite transmitter,' Hamish said. 'Latest technology. We strap it to her back, a bit like a mini rucksack. It tells us her position. You know, where she is in the world. We can tell how high she's flying and how fast. We can follow her journey all the way to Africa and back.'

'Brilliant,' I said.

'Isn't it a bit heavy?' frowned Iona.

'No. Here, feel it.'

Hamish handed it to Iona. She held it in her palm and curled her fingers around it.

'But how can *we* find out where she's been,' I asked.

'I'll give you a special code,' he said. 'You put it into your computer and it plots her journey on Google Earth. You might even be able to see which tree she roosts in.'

'So we can actually see her fly?' asked Iona.

'No,' said Hamish. 'Google Earth has satellite pictures of the Earth that were taken before now, but you can see the sort of places she flies over.'

The osprey jabbed at the leather gloves with her beak while Hamish tied the straps of the transmitter. 'No one must find out about this nest,' said Hamish. 'Not a soul. News like this has the nasty habit of finding the wrong ears.

Sky Hawk

Some people pay thousands to get their hands on osprey eggs.'

'We've kept her secret this long, haven't we?' said Iona suddenly fierce.

Hamish grinned. 'You have,' he said. He passed her a small tin. 'And she wouldn't be here now if it wasn't for you. So you get to choose her coloured leg ring, Iona.'

Iona probed around in the tin, sifting through the coloured rings.

'Take your time, Iona!' I said. 'Her eggs will have hatched by the time you choose one.'

She frowned at me. 'It's got to be right.' She picked up different rings, examining each one as if it were a precious stone. 'Here . . . ' she pulled out a white ring with the letters, RS.

'Why RS?' I said.

'RS . . . it sounds a bit like Iris,' said Iona. 'We'll call her Iris, after the Greek goddess of the wind and sky.'

'What?'

'Don't you remember? We did it in school. Iris was a messenger from heaven.'

'It's not a very Scottish name,' I said. 'This is a Scottish bird.'

Iona frowned at me. 'And what makes her so Scottish if

she spends half the year in another country?'

Hamish clipped the ring on her leg and laughed. 'You're like an old married couple, bickering away.'

'Iona wins,' Dad chuckled. 'Iris, it is.'

I scowled at him.

'So, Iona,' said Hamish, 'do you want to do the honours and let Iris go?'

Iona looked at me. 'I think Callum should do it.'

'You mean it?' I said. I couldn't believe it.

Iona smiled at me and nodded. 'We both saved her.'

'All right then,' said Hamish. 'Here you are, Callum, you don't need gloves on. Hold her like this.'

I wrapped my hands around the osprey's folded wings. The top feathers were smooth and soft, but I could feel the quills of the flight feathers like strong wire under my fingers.

'Hold her firm, mind,' said Hamish. 'Face into the wind and just throw her, as high as you can.'

I turned Iris into the wind. Her whole body tensed under my hands. Her muscles were tight and hard. The wind ruffled the soft feathers on her head. She fixed her eyes on the sky above.

'Now,' said Hamish.

I threw her upwards. She exploded from my hands in a

Sky Hawk

blur of wing and feather. I felt the rush of air against my face as she beat her wings.

Up, she flew, into the sunlight.

A single feather spiralled down to earth.

She was free.

CHAPTER 13

I returned Rob's bike the next morning.

'I've cleaned your bike,' I said.

Rob was down in the village with Euan and some boys from school. They were kicking a ball about on the rough stony ground below the play park.

Rob glanced down at his bike. 'It's not just some cheap bike, that. Dad nearly killed me when I didn't come home with it last night.'

'I know,' I said. 'I'm sorry.'

'What did *she* want, anyway?' said Rob.

'Who, Iona?' I said. I shrugged my shoulders. 'It was nothing.'

'We waited for ages but you never came back,' said Rob. 'Where d'you go? What were you doing?'

Sky Hawk

'It wasn't anything,' I said irritably. 'Just drop it OK?'

'Hey, Callum,' shouted Euan, 'we need a goalie, are you playing?'

Euan kicked the ball to me but I let it roll past and into a ditch.

'Or maybe you want to get back to your girlfriend?' said Rob.

I grabbed him by his coat. 'Shut up, Rob,' I yelled.

Our faces were inches apart.

'She's a nutter,' said Rob. 'You said so yourself.'

Something inside me snapped.

I punched him, right in the face.

Rob scrambled up and launched at me. We sprawled over his bike, punching and kicking. I felt the crack of his bike computer splitting open beneath my back. Then Euan was there, pulling Rob away before the other boys could crowd around us.

'Go, Callum,' Euan said. He held Rob by the arm. 'Just go.'

Rob and I glared at each other. I couldn't tell if it was hurt or hate in his eyes, but I didn't care. I turned and walked up the road out of the village and didn't look back.

* * *

When I reached the loch, Dad's Land Rover was parked on the far shore near the tree house. Iona was sitting on the bonnet drinking from a steaming mug.

A thick moustache of hot chocolate sat upon her top lip. 'What've you done to your face?' she said.

I wiped my sleeve along my mouth. It left a trail of blood, mud, and saliva. 'Nothing,' I said.

She passed me a paper tissue and I tried to clean most of it off. There was hammering and banging from the branches above.

'Your dad thought our tree could do with a bit of improvement,' said Iona.

'You told him about it?' I said.

Iona nodded. 'He knows about the ospreys,' she said, 'so it makes no difference.'

I could just see Dad's feet through the leaves. I thought at first the hammering might scare the ospreys, but when I looked across to the island I could just see the head of Iris poking up from the nest, watching us.

'The ospreys think your dad's a strange big bird,' Iona laughed. 'Have you seen what he's doing up there?'

I climbed up Dad's ladder into the tree. Wooden planks of all shapes and sizes were balanced in the branches. Graham and Hamish were up in the tree too. They'd built a wide platform support and were now building up the sides of the tree-house.

'What d'you think, Callum?' said Dad.

'Really great,' I said, looking around. And it was. Dad, Hamish, and Graham had built it around the main trunk. I could already see it was going to be huge. 'I could live up here.'

'That's the general idea, Cal,' said Graham. 'It's Mum and Dad's way of getting rid of you.'

I grinned at him. He was just putting the hinges on the trapdoor in the base of the tree-house. 'Thanks, Graham,' I said. And I really meant it.

We stopped work for lunch. Dad drove us back to the farmhouse in the Land Rover, all squashed together along the front seat. A fine rain misted the windscreen and hid the hills from view. Iona stretched her bare feet on the dashboard and warmed her toes in the hot air from the vents.

'Come on in,' said Mum, 'you're all soaked, the lot of you.'

We all piled into the kitchen, our damp clothes steaming in the warm air.

'You'll stay for lunch, Hamish, won't you?' said Mum. 'And what about you, Iona. Will you stay?'

Iona nodded. 'Yes please, Mrs McGregor.'

'Shall I ring your grandad?' said Mum.

'I will,' said Iona. She took the phone out into the hall.

Mum turned to me. 'That's a fair nasty cut on your lip, Callum,' she said.

I put my fingers to the split lip where Rob had punched me. It felt swollen and sore. 'Fell off my bike,' I said. I looked at her and could tell she knew it was a lie.

'Go and clean yourself up, then,' she said. 'And wash your hands.'

As I went to the bathroom, I found Iona on the stairs with the phone in her hands.

'You've not rung him, have you?' I said.

'Don't tell your mum, will you?'

'Won't he wonder where you are?' I said.

She shook her head and frowned.

'He forgets things, does Grandad. Anyway, he's probably asleep.'

For lunch Mum gave us roast lamb, roast potatoes, carrots, and peas and thick brown gravy. I thought I had a good appetite, but Iona had seconds of everything and then thirds. She even managed a huge bowl of Mum's best treacle pudding and custard.

Hamish flopped down in the saggy sofa by the cooking

range. He closed his eyes and folded his hands on his stomach. 'That was so good,' he groaned. 'I won't be able to move for a week.'

'Aye, well, there's not much point going anywhere,' said Dad. 'The rain's set to stay.'

I looked out across the yard. Even the barn was hidden by a thick curtain of rain. Gusts of wind smattered the raindrops against the window. Not even the thought of going to see the ospreys was enough to make me want to go outside.

Iona and I packed the dishwasher, while Mum cleared the table.

'I wish I lived on a farm,' said Iona. 'My grandad had a farm, didn't he?'

'That's right,' said Mum. 'Your grandad and Callum's granda knew each other well.'

Iona eyes widened. 'Did they?'

Mum nodded. 'They were friends and rivals. They both bred Scottish Blackface sheep and showed them at all the big shows.'

'I didn't know that,' I said.

Mum hung the wet tea-towels to dry. 'I've got a box of Granda's old photos up in the attic,' she said. 'I'll see if I can find them.'

Iona and I sat at the kitchen table with our backs to the radiator and waited for her while she searched the attic.

'Here they are,' Mum said. She put an old cardboard box on the table. It smelt musty, of mice and mothballs. 'No one's looked at these for years.'

Mum pulled out big brown envelopes and looked inside. 'There you go,' she said with a big smile. 'That's the two of them, side by side.'

It was a black and white photo of an agricultural show dated 1962. There was a line of farmers holding sheep waiting to be judged.

'Don't they look young?' said Mum. 'That's your grandad there.'

Iona stared into the photo. 'He looks really happy there, doesn't he?'

Mum smiled. 'You can keep it if you like.'

Iona and I looked through more photos. There were lots of the farm and people in strange old-fashioned clothes. Even Mum didn't know who some of them were.

I looked across at Iona. She was holding a photo in her hand. I could tell it was really old, it was brown and faded. I couldn't get a clear view, but Iona's eyes were shining.

'You're not going to believe this, Callum,' she said, holding up the photo. 'You're really not.'

CHAPTER 14

'Amazing,' said Dad. 'I never knew about this.'

'Incredible!' said Hamish.

I peered over Iona's shoulder at the faded photo in her hand. It was a photo of a loch, our loch, dated 1905. There was the rocky island and a cluster of trees, not just pines but small wind-bent trees and bushes too. But there, unmistakably, on the tallest pine was a huge tangle of sticks. It was so obviously an eyrie, much bigger than the one Iris and her mate had built.

'I can't believe we've had ospreys on this farm before,' said Dad, 'over a hundred years ago.'

'They must've been about the last,' said Hamish. 'There were no recorded nests at all in Scotland between about 1910 and the early 1950s.'

Mum shook her head. 'I don't know how people can shoot them, or steal their eggs.'

'For private collections and for money,' said Hamish. 'Some people will do it today if given half a chance. Some people poison them because they think they take too many fish.'

'That's just sick,' said Dad.

'We've got to keep our nest secret,' said Iona. 'All of us.'

'You're right there,' said Hamish. 'Letting people see ospreys at protected reserves is important. But the only way to build up osprey numbers is at nests like this one, nests kept secret and hidden away.'

'Well, I think Granda would be well pleased with you, Iona,' said Graham with a grin. 'We'll make you an honorary member of the farm.'

You'd have thought Graham had given her a slice of the sun, by the way Iona smiled back.

'Talking of grandads,' said Mum, 'I think your grandad will be worrying where you are.'

'I'll give you a lift home,' said Hamish, 'I ought to go.'

Mum packed Iona off with some thick socks and a fleece jacket I'd grown out of. She wrapped up half a fruit cake too. When Iona said no, Mum said it was too much for Dad to eat, said he was fat enough already. Dad winked at Iona and patted his belly and Iona laughed.

It didn't stop raining that day. After Iona had gone I went to my bedroom and rummaged under my bed for an old scrapbook I was given a few years ago. I'd only put in a few monster cards I'd collected back then. I stripped them out and wrote in big letters 'The Ospreys on our Farm'.

Maybe I could keep a record of them for other people in a hundred years' time. And then I wrote in smaller letters, 'The Diary of Iris'.

I logged onto my computer and typed in the code Hamish had given us for Iris. It was amazing. On Google Earth, it put her position exactly on the island on the loch. 17.00 GMT. Hamish said GMT was Greenwich Mean Time, London time. I looked out of the window and shivered. I knew Iris would be sitting on her eggs. There was no shelter for her there.

I wanted to write her position, her coordinates, in the scrapbook, but something stopped me. I just couldn't do it. It was as if writing it out would somehow give away our secret. So I stuck in some photos that Hamish had given me and just wrote, '17.00 GMT. Nest site, Secret Location. Scotland.'

I lay back on my bed and listened to the rain. I closed my eyes and tried to imagine myself high on that eyrie. I tried to imagine the raindrops sliding across my oiled feathers and the sway of the eyrie in the wind coming down from the rain-hammered mountains.

Iris spread her wings across the nest. The rain ran down her long flight feathers and soaked through the tangle of sticks to the dark rain-stained branches. The eggs were warm and dry beneath her, sheltered in their bed of moss and soft down feathers.

The fibres of the tree creaked and groaned as the gale thrashed against it. Iris could feel the changing patterns of air around her, and the pressure of the storm, deep and hollow. Her bones and chest ached with it. She gripped her talons into the knot of sticks, and pressed herself deeper against her clutch of eggs.

One foot was still sore. She flinched at the memory of the humans holding her. They had touched her and unfurled her wings. The boy had looked deep into her eyes and she had stared back, mapping the strange contours of his face.

Now Iris sat tight in the eyrie, in the howling wind and hurting rain. The valley was human-less again. The acrid breath of their machine had long blown away across the hillside.

Yet the boy remained in her memory, the boy who held her and eased her pain. He had given back her sky. Somewhere deep inside her, Iris folded the landscape of his face into the mountains, skies, and rivers of her soul.

CHAPTER 15

I was glad when the summer holidays started. It meant I could spend most of the time with Iona at the loch. Rob and I had hardly spoken. I'd offered him twenty pounds towards the bike computer that had broken in our fight, but he didn't take it. He said he wished he hadn't wasted his time picking a fight with a loser like me. I couldn't be bothered with him, either. I did feel bad about Euan, though. Euan asked if he could fish on our loch, like he did each summer, but I put him off with some poor excuses. I didn't want to risk anyone seeing the ospreys.

So Iona and I went to the tree-house most days. Dad and Graham had finished the house with Hamish's help. Boards and planks of wood had been nailed together to build up the sides, and the roof was made from a piece of corrugated iron from an old pig pen. There were big draughty gaps we stuffed with sacking and tied with baler twine. Dad had put two stools next to the wide window with its wooden shutters that overlooked the loch and the mountains. He'd built a shelf and put in a big wooden trunk we used as a table and a store to keep our bird books and Iona's paints and notebooks. Graham camouflaged the sloping roof with old ivy and dead branches, so it was almost impossible to see from the outside. It was perfect.

I hauled myself up through the trapdoor into the tree-house.

'Did you remember the drawing pins?' said Iona.

'Yes,' I said. 'Better still, I've brought food. Mum made us some sandwiches. What d'you want drawing pins for, anyway?'

Iona swept her hand around the tree-house. 'We've got to decorate it,' she said. 'Make it ours.'

'What with?' I said.

'I'm going to stick up some of the sketches I've done, of the ospreys. Here,' she said handing me a wodge of drawings. 'This was when the chick was little.'

I looked at a drawing dated nineteenth of June. There was one scruffy chick sticking its head above the eyrie. It was only a couple of weeks old then. I remembered that day so clearly. It was the first time we actually got a glimpse of it. But we were also sad because we knew then that the other two eggs hadn't hatched.

'I can't believe how much it's grown since then,' I said. I pinned the picture up on the wooden walls of the tree-house next to a later picture of the chick being fed by Iris.

'And this is the one I've done today,' said Iona. She held up a new painting dated second of August. It showed the chick stretching its wings. It was almost as big as its parents now and there wasn't much room in the nest any more when it flapped about. Its feathers were still a mottled cream and brown, and its eyes were deep amber, not yellow.

'Look,' said Iona, pointing out of the window. 'It's having another go.'

We sat looking out across the loch. The eyrie was bright in the late morning sunshine. I reached into my bag for my binoculars.

'I thought you said you brought sandwiches,' said Iona. 'I'm starving.'

I threw her a packet of sandwiches, propped my elbows on the window ledge and focused my binoculars on the eyrie.

The chick stood on the edge of the eyrie, flapping its huge wings, testing the wind. It lifted slightly off the nest, hovering just above it. We could hear the call of one of its parents in another tree, encouraging it.

'Go on,' whispered Iona.

It dropped down onto the eyrie again, standing right on the very edge. Then, as if it had made up its mind, it spread its wings and launched up into the air, followed by a downward plummet towards the loch.

I held my breath.

The chick beat its wings, flapping hard. It swooped up from the loch and flew in a wide arc up over the trees. Round and round it flew, above the woodland, flap, flap, flap, with its big wings, trying to keep airborne. We watched it try to land on a thin branch of a tree near the eyrie, but the branch bowed and bent beneath it. It took off again, flapping towards the eyrie this time. Its long gangly legs were outstretched and it wobbled in the air like a helicopter on a really windy day. It mistimed its landing, crashed into the nest and then sat up, ruffling its feathers back into place.

'Flying's the easy bit,' I laughed. 'It's the landing that's difficult.'

Iona smiled. 'Time for a new picture,' she said. She reached into the trunk for her box of art stuff.

'Where d'you get all those paints?' I asked. She had more tins and pots than I'd ever seen her with before.

Sky Hawk

'Mrs Wicklow was cleaning out the art room and dropped them round for my birthday,' she said.

'I didn't know it was your birthday,' I said.

'Well, it's next week,' said Iona. 'But I couldn't wait to use the paints.'

Iona found a new sheet of paper and started sketching.

I glanced at the picture. I thought she'd do one of the chick's first flight, but instead she was drawing Iris on a tree on the other side of the loch.

'Hamish thinks she'll set off to Africa soon,' said Iona.

I looked out across the loch where Iris sat in a tall dead tree. She was bright against the dark woodland.

'Iris always sits on that far tree now, doesn't she?' I said.

'I think she looks sad,' said Iona.

'She's a bird,' I said. 'How can she look sad?'

Iona shrugged her shoulders and kept working at her picture. 'She does to me,' said Iona. 'She knows she can't stay however much she wants to. She can't help it. She'll leave her chick and go.'

I laughed. 'She won't even think about it.'

Iona crumpled up her picture and flung it across the floor. She stormed down the hatch and away from the tree-house.

'Iona,' I called, but she had already disappeared into the trees.

I caught up with her by the river. She was sitting on a stone, hunched over, digging her penknife into something in her hand.

'She'll be back, Iona,' I said.

Iona turned round. Tears streaked down her cheeks. 'Will she?'

The gold locket lay open in her palm. Deep scratches were cut into the photo of her mother's face.

I sat down close beside her. 'Your ma will come back for you, Iona,' I said.

Iona snapped the locket shut and wiped the tears from her face. 'No,' she said. She shook her head. 'She's never coming back, for me.'

CHAPTER 16

I told Mum about Iona's birthday and she insisted on making a cake. I'd told her not to fuss, but a week later we were sitting round the kitchen table singing Iona 'Happy Birthday' and watching her blow out the candles on her cake.

'Did you make a wish?' said Mum.

Iona nodded and cut the cake. The candles trailed their wisps of black smoke up into the air. 'Can't tell you what it is, or it won't come true,' she said. She held up the first piece of cake, 'Who wants some?'

Hamish reached across the kitchen table. 'I'll have a piece,' he said, 'in exchange for this.' He handed Iona a parcel wrapped in shiny paper.

'For me?' she said. She tore the wrapping open, her eyes

shining. 'Wow, a book on birds of prey, thanks, Hamish.'

'And we've got you a little something,' said Mum.

Dad lifted out a large parcel from under the table. 'This is for you. We hope you like them.'

'I've never had so many presents,' said Iona. She unwrapped the parcel and opened the box inside. 'Thanks!'

I looked inside the box and almost choked. Mum had bought Iona a pair of pink walking boots, with purple laces. 'They're really gross,' I said.

But Iona held the boots up, a huge grin on her face. 'I love them,' she said. 'I really love them.'

Mum passed Iona some socks. 'These are for you, too. Try the boots on, see if they fit.'

Iona pulled the socks on and slid her feet into the boots. 'They're perfect,' she said. 'How did you know what size to get?'

Mum glanced at Dad and smiled. 'It was his idea,' she said. 'He measured the footprints of your bare feet in the mud.'

Graham helped himself to a second piece of cake. 'Sorry I didn't get you anything, Iona. Tell you what! I'll treat you to a rally drive round the farm on the back of the quad bike.'

'No you won't!' snapped Mum.

Sky Hawk

Graham shoved the cake in his mouth and winked at Iona.

Mum poured cups of tea and put some more cakes on the table. 'It's a shame your grandad couldn't come round as well.'

Iona nodded, prodding at the sticky crumbs on her plate with a finger. 'He had things to do.'

I knew she didn't want Mum asking questions. 'Why don't you try out your new boots?' I said.

'Can I?' said Iona.

'Go on,' smiled Dad. 'Why don't you and Callum go on up the hill?'

I went to get my boots and followed Iona out into the yard. She was bouncing up and down on the spot, waiting for me.

'You don't really like them do you?' I said. 'They're pink!'

Iona walked on, balancing on hardened ridges of mud. 'Pink's my favourite colour.'

I frowned at her. 'You never said.'

She laughed. 'You never asked.'

I gave her a shove into a sticky mud puddle and ran ahead.

'Hey, watch it,' she shouted. 'I don't want them getting dirty.'

We ran up the steepest part of the hill to the stone wall

running along the top edge of the field. The sun was hot on our backs and we were out of breath when we reached the wall. Sheep were scattered across the ridge dividing our farm from the valley beyond with the loch and the ospreys.

Iona licked her finger and tried to rub mud off the front of one boot. 'I wish it wasn't school next week,' she said.

'Me too,' I said. It would feel different back at school, I knew it would.

'It's only the middle of August,' said Iona. 'When I was in London, the schools didn't go back until September.'

I picked up small stones and tried flinging them as far as I could down the hill. 'That's Scotland for you,' I said.

'You know what we should do before we go back to school?' said Iona.

'What?' I turned to look at her. She had a huge grin on her face.

'Stay a night in the tree-house.'

'Mum would never let me,' I said.

'Don't tell her,' said Iona. 'Grandad won't notice me gone. We'll both sneak out and meet there.'

I thought of sleeping in the tree-house, in the darkness with all the noises of the night around us, waking up and seeing the dawn. We'd talked about it before, but never seriously. Now it seemed like the best idea.

Sky Hawk

'All right,' I said. 'This Saturday, you're on.'

Iona smiled. 'Don't come up till then,' she said, 'I have to get something ready for then, a surprise.'

'What?' I said.

She laughed. 'You'll just have to wait and see.'

I turned to head down the hill, but Iona called me back.

'Callum,' she said.

I looked at her.

'Today,' she said. 'All of it. It's been the best.'

I grinned at her. 'Come on,' I yelled. 'Race you.'

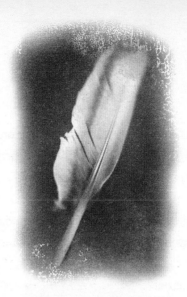

CHAPTER 17

That Saturday I packed my rucksack with two sleeping bags, a couple of torches, one of Mum's fruit cakes and some crisps I'd raided from the kitchen. I planned to meet Iona at the tree-house, go home for tea, and then slip out after dark.

'Planning on running away?' said Mum.

Did she know? I looked at her but she was smiling.

'You look like you're going away for a week,' she said.

I slipped round the other side of the kitchen table. 'It's just stuff for the tree-house,' I said.

'Aye, well don't be long,' she said. 'There's rain coming. This hot weather's going to break soon.'

'I'll be back for tea,' I said.

I walked out of the cool kitchen into the wall of thick

summer heat. The air was still with it. The farm dogs, Kip and Elsie, lay panting in the shelter of their kennels. I turned on the hose and they chomped on the sparkling stream of water as it splashed into their bowls. Sheep were pressed into the shade of the stone wall along the top fields. The grass was brown and dry and small insects buzzed above the grass flower heads.

I was glad to reach the shade of the trees along the path by the loch.

I'd been thinking about the surprise Iona said she'd have for me. Was she waiting for me? Watching me?

I looked up to the trapdoor into the tree-house. It was shut. 'Iona?' I called.

No answer. I climbed the rope ladder and pushed open the trapdoor, half expecting to see her face grinning at me. 'Iona, it's me,' I called again.

I hauled my rucksack up into the tree-house and looked around. Iona wasn't there, but on the wooden wall opposite the window was Iona's surprise. It was a huge painting of an osprey catching a fish. It was painted onto the wood itself. It was so detailed down to every feather. There were drips of spilled paint along the floor below it. It must've taken her ages to do.

I pulled the cake and crisps from my rucksack and put

them on the table, and rolled the sleeping bags out across the floor.

'Iona?' I lifted up the bench store to see if she was hiding, but she wasn't anywhere. I leaned out of the window to look back along the footpath. There was no sign of her.

The clouds had turned purple and grey, like a dark bruise spreading across the sky. To the south, thunder rumbled over the mountains. If Iona didn't get here soon, she'd be soaked. Maybe she'd forgotten, but it wasn't like her.

I scrambled down the rope ladder and set off along the path hoping to meet Iona on the way. I followed the track by the river to join the old mineral tracks going down to the village. In the crook of a dried-up puddle lay a long feather caked in dirt. I crouched down to pick it up and clean it on my sleeve. It was creamy white with thick stripes of dark brown, an osprey feather.

I tucked it in the combat pocket of my shorts. Large, single drops of rain hit the ground by my feet sending little puffs of dust into the air. I glanced up at the sky. A great cloud was looming up over the ridge, its shadow dark against the hillside. The thunder sounded again, closer this time. I began to run. The sky was darkening, and as I reached the road into the village even the streetlights lit up.

I could see Iona's house on the edge of the village. It was

Sky Hawk

a small squat cottage, painted in whitewash that had turned grey over the years. An old crofter's cottage lay derelict beside it. Maybe I'd missed Iona on the way here. Maybe she was at the tree-house already. But I was sure I hadn't missed her. I knew she'd take this path, I just knew it.

I jogged along the road to the house and slowed to a walk near the open gate. The front garden was a mass of weeds and tall grasses. An old bed frame lay in the corner strangled in bindweed, its rusty springs and tattered cover decorated by the white trumpet-shaped flowers.

A dim light came from within the house. I'd never been inside before. Rob and I used to dare each other to knock on the door and run away. We'd hide in the bushes and watch Mad Old McNair shake his sticks wildly in the air from his doorway.

What if Iona wasn't there?

I could feel my heart thumping in my chest.

I walked up the path and stopped at the door. The pale blue paint was peeled and flaking.

I knocked on the door and waited.

It opened just a crack.

I could see Iona's grandad, the white bristles on his face, a reddened eye and the sleeve of his dressing gown.

'What d'you want?' His breath stank of whisky.

I wanted to run. 'Is Iona in?'

He squinted at me through the door. 'Callum McGregor, is it?'

'It is, Mr McNair.'

He opened the door a bit wider. 'Come in, if you like. You cannae stay long. Iona's not well. Summer flu it is. Had it meself back along.'

I followed him into the front room. I had to squeeze past piles and piles of boxes and old newspapers. The room smelt damp and musty, like spoiled grain. Thin brown curtains were drawn across the window and a television flickered silently in the corner. Iona was curled up in an armchair under some blankets. She looked cold despite the heat of the day. A mug of tea with a scum of cold milk and a plate of uneaten toast were on the floor beside her.

Iona's grandad glared at me from under his thick eyebrows. 'Don't be long now.' He picked up a half empty bottle of whisky and shuffled past. 'I'm away to bed, Iona. Call me if you need me.'

I sat down on a pile of old newspapers next to her.

'Hi, Iona,' I said. 'You OK?'

'I woke up with flu this morning,' she said. She wiped her nose across a scrunched up tissue on the armchair.

I passed her a box of clean tissues from the floor.

Sky Hawk

'Thanks,' she said. She lay back and pinched her fingers on her forehead.

'Feels like my head's about to explode. I just couldn't make it to the tree-house. Sorry.'

'Doesn't matter,' I said. 'Another time.'

Iona screwed her eyes tight shut. I could tell she was trying not to cry. I knew she must be feeling pretty rough, because I didn't think she'd miss out on sleeping in the tree-house for anything.

'The painting's really good,' I said, 'of the osprey.'

'You like it?'

I nodded. I took the feather from my pocket. 'I found this for you,' I said.

'Osprey feather,' she murmured. 'Where did you find it?'

I started telling Iona, but I could tell she wasn't really listening. Her eyes were closing and she was drifting into sleep. I sat there watching the silent people on the TV. Iona's breaths were short and shallow. I heard the creak of floorboards and the dull thump of Iona's grandad climbing into bed in the room above.

I tucked the feather into the crook of her hand and got up to leave.

'Bye, Iona,' I whispered.

'Callum?'

'Yes?' I said.

'Look after Iris. Keep her safe.'

'You can check on her yourself tomorrow,' I said.

'Promise me.'

Iona looked at me through tired eyes.

'Yes, Iona,' I said. 'Of course, I promise.'

I pulled the blankets up around her and left after that.

Outside the weather broke. Rain hammered the hot cement. Sheet lightning flashed neon yellow.

I walked home through the monsoon rain.

I never saw Iona again.

CHAPTER 18

I woke to rain pattering on my bedroom window. I glanced at my clock; it was nine already. I'd slept late. I pulled on my clothes and peered out of the window. It had rained in the night, hard and heavy. Deep puddles pooled across the yard. Kip and Elsie were barking in their kennel. I looked at the clock again and thought it was strange because Dad usually let them out by now.

I went down to the kitchen and Mum turned to me as I opened the door. Dad, Graham, and Hamish were there too. Graham slammed his cup down and stormed out. Dad and Hamish wouldn't look at me. Were they cross? Did they know about the plan to sleep in the tree-house?

'Sit down, Callum,' said Mum.

'What have I done?'

Mum put her arms round me. 'It's Iona,' she said. Mum held me so tight. 'She died . . . last night.'

I pushed Mum away. 'No. But I saw her. I saw her last night.'

Dad came over to me. 'I'm sorry . . . '

'It's not true,' I yelled. 'She was OK. She's got summer flu, that's all, just flu.' I looked at Hamish. He looked pale, deathly white.

'I've just come from her house,' he said. 'The ambulance was there.'

I backed away from them to the door, shoved my boots on and started running. Running and running. My lungs burned and my chest ached but I didn't stop until I reached the tree-house.

I pulled up on the rope ladder. My hands stung with cold and my feet slipped on the wet wooden rungs. I flung open the trapdoor above me and hauled myself in. Rain had seeped into every part of the tree-house. Water dripped from the sleeping bags and the cake on the table was soggy and turned to mush. The colours in Iona's osprey painting had bled onto the floor. All the tiny details were lost. It was a ghost osprey now.

I kicked a box of biscuits out through the trapdoor and watched it clatter against the tree roots. I wanted to scream and shout. I wanted to cry. But the tears just couldn't come.

I flung open the shutters and the north wind slammed them against the wooden sides. I leaned out of the window.

'Iona's dead,' I shouted, 'dead.'

Iris turned to look in my direction. She was hunkered down on the sheltered side of her nesting tree. The mottled brown of her wings merged into the peeling bark of the branch. Her mate was in the eyrie. I couldn't see the fledgling chick, but knew it must be huddled in there somewhere trying to keep dry.

I leaned right out of the window so half of me was over the drop below. 'She's dead,' I shouted, 'dead! But what do you know? You're only a stupid bird.'

Iris ruffled her feathers, her bright eyes watching me. Her alarm call rang out through the driving rain. 'Kee, kee, kee.'

I clapped my hands together and Iris launched into the air. 'You're only a stupid, dumb bird.'

I slammed the shutter against the wooden sides of the tree-house and the noise echoed across the loch. Iris wheeled away over the wooded hillside behind me, the underside of her body pale against the iron sky.

I sat there staring out over the loch, just staring. Broken sunlight filtered through the clouds. Iris didn't return to the nest. Iona had said she would leave for her wintering grounds in Africa by the end of the week. Maybe she had already gone. I had promised Iona I'd look after Iris, and now I'd scared her away.

I was half asleep when a soft rush of feathers whistled over my head followed by a dull thump. Iris landed on a branch beside the tree-house. I could hardly breathe. She was so close. I could see the vane of every feather and the metallic curve of each talon. She ruffled her feathers and scanned the southern horizon.

'You're going, aren't you?' I whispered.

She turned her head, and fixed me with her brilliant yellow eyes. She looked right into me. And suddenly I knew then, in that one moment, I was as much part of her world as she was of mine. I couldn't help thinking that maybe, just maybe, deep in her bird soul, she knew the promise I had given to Iona.

Iris flew up, through the broken sunlight into the cold clear air. She circled the nest one last time. Her mate was preening his feathers, oiling them after the heavy rains. She banked away from the eyrie they had built from sticks and grasses, and away from the insistent calls of the full-grown chick they had reared that summer.

The pull south was too great now. The need to fly was strong. It pulsed inside, hard-wired deep into every nerve and muscle and cell. Each day, the sun did not rise so high. Each day its arc across the sky lowered towards the pale blue curve of the southern horizon.

Iris soared on the updraught of the cold north wind. It rippled under her feathers and carried her up, through the drifting threads of cloud. This was her world, of vast skies and reflected waters. She flew high into the fast-winds, leaving behind the ancient landscape of mountain peaks, glittering lochs, and wide river valleys.

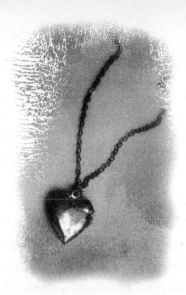

CHAPTER 19

The church was cool inside. I sat in silence between Rob and Euan while they talked across me, and watched golden specks of dust drift in the sunbeams from the high windows.

'Have you taken your antibiotics?' said Rob.

'Taste horrible, don't they?' whispered Euan. 'Mum's terrified I'm going to drop dead from meningitis too. She won't leave me alone.'

Rob nodded. 'My mum's the same, keeps taking my temperature every five minutes. I can't believe we've had nearly the first two weeks off school.'

It was a memorial service for Iona. Mum and Dad sat behind me and I could see Hamish sitting near the front. Teachers, children, and parents from school filled the little church. Feet scraped on the stone floor and voices rose up into the eaves. I dug my nails into my hands and waited.

Silence fell across the church as Reverend Parsons walked up the aisle followed slowly by old Mr McNair. A woman shuffled next to him, her arm linked with his. It was Iona's mother. I recognized her from the photo in Iona's locket, but here her face looked grey and lined, her dark eyes sunk deep in their sockets. I couldn't imagine she was ever a dancer. She kept her head down as if she could feel all the eyes in church upon her.

Reverend Parsons helped them into their seats and climbed up into his eagle-winged pulpit. My thoughts were running with Iona through the hills as his voice carried over our heads. Two girls from the class read out poems and one sang a solo. Then we all sang 'All Things Bright and Beautiful', which had been Iona's favourite hymn, once.

When the service ended, we all stood as Mr McNair and Iona's mother walked back out of the church. They stopped when they reached my pew. Iona's mother turned to me. Her hands were clasped as if in prayer, and they were shaking badly. Her skin was papery white and covered in dark spidery bruises.

'Callum McGregor?' she said.

Her voice was thin and hoarse as if it was a struggle to speak.

I nodded.

'I think this belongs to you now.'

She cupped my hand in hers and dropped a small heart-shaped locket and chain into my hand. It was the gold locket Iona always wore around her neck. I'd never seen her without it. Iona's mother squeezed my hand and turned away.

I flicked open the locket, then wished I hadn't. On one side was the picture of Iona and on the other side, in the small heart-shaped space, was a photo of me, a small photo I recognized from a class picture at school. I shoved the locket and chain deep in my pocket, feeling angry at Rob and Euan for watching and angrier at Iona for even putting me in there.

'Look at the state of her,' said Euan's mum, watching Iona's mother leave the church. 'It's enough to make your heart bleed.'

'The shame of it,' said Rob's mum behind us, 'letting a wee bairn like Iona live with that old man. He was half drunk on whisky most of the time, didn't have the wit to see she was so ill.'

Mum rounded on them both. I don't think I'd ever seen

her so angry. 'Aye, and who carries that shame? Fiona was our friend once, remember? What did we do to keep an eye out for her little girl? Did Mr McNair feel he could call on any of us?'

Mum reached in her bag and thrust the car keys in Dad's hands. 'I'm walking home,' she snapped. 'I need some fresh air.'

She stormed out of the church and I followed her out into the car park and up the road out of the village. We walked in silence, Mum marching ahead, her shoes click clacking on the road.

We were almost at the bottom of the farm track when Dad pulled up beside us in the car. We climbed in and he drove us the last bit home.

'Sorry I snapped,' said Mum. 'I can't stop thinking I should have done more for them all.'

'I know,' said Dad. 'It's how everyone else is feeling too.'

Dad pulled up in the yard and I climbed out of the car. My legs felt like lead. I was so tired.

Dad caught up with me as I crossed the yard. 'I've just been talking to Euan's mum,' he said. 'Euan's been quite upset about not seeing you over the summer.'

I shrugged my shoulders.

'Euan's always been a good friend to you,' said Dad.

I kicked my boots off and pushed open the kitchen door.

'I've invited him round,' Dad said. 'His mum's bringing him.'

'I don't want anyone round.'

'School starts tomorrow,' said Dad. 'It'll do you good to see him before then.'

I pushed my way past Mum in the kitchen. 'I'll be in my room.'

'I told Euan you'd take him fishing,' called Dad. 'He hasn't been all summer. I said you'd take him up on the loch.'

I spun round. 'Not the loch! Are you stupid?'

'That's enough, Callum,' said Dad.

'But the ospreys, we said we'd keep them secret,' I yelled.

'You need your friends, more than you think,' said Dad. 'Don't turn your back on them. If you don't take Euan fishing on the loch, I will.'

CHAPTER 20

I stormed upstairs into my room. I was furious with Dad. I didn't want anyone round. I heard a car engine in the distance and looked out of the window to see a car coming up the farm track. It pulled up in the yard and I watched as Euan climbed out of the back, followed by Rob. He was here too.

'Callum, they're here,' Mum shouted.

I shut the door and pressed my back against it.

'What you doing, Callum?'

I could hear voices in the kitchen below.

I changed into a T-shirt and old shorts. The locket fell out of my trousers as I slung them over the chair. I scooped it up, slipped it into the case of my binoculars and put it on top of the wardrobe.

Mum opened my door. 'Euan and Rob are here,' she said.

I scowled at her. 'I know. I heard you.'

Euan and Rob were waiting for me in the kitchen. Euan's box of fishing tackle and rods were on the table.

'Euan's looking forward to this,' said his mum, 'aren't you, Euan?'

I looked across at him and he fumbled with the straps on his fishing case.

'We won't have much time,' I said. 'It's nearly five already.'

Mum passed me my rucksack. 'Dad'll take you up to the loch in the Land Rover,' she said. 'I've packed some sandwiches and cake in here for you all.'

We climbed in the back of the Land Rover and sat in silence as Dad drove us up to the loch. Life jackets and oars were packed around our feet.

Dad pulled up by the gritty shore of the loch. 'I've got some work to do up here,' said Dad. 'So you can take the boat out if you like.'

I jumped out and scanned the sky. There was no sign of the male osprey and the chick. I knew they would be somewhere around. Hamish said the males and young birds didn't leave for Africa until mid September.

'Come on, Callum,' said Dad.

Sky Hawk

We all helped haul the small boat into the water. Euan loaded his fishing gear, we jumped in and Dad pushed us off.

'See you later,' Dad yelled.

I stared after him to the shore. A few late mayflies danced in the shallows and sunlight sparkled in the ripples from the boat. We spun in a slow arc, bobbing gently in the water. The air was warm and still in the shelter of the trees.

Euan looked out across the loch. 'I reckon we'll have to row out to the far end of the loch,' he called out. 'There's a breeze out there on the water. Good day for a Bristol Black Hopper.'

'The junior fly fishing champion has spoken,' said Rob giving me a nudge.

I scowled and turned my back on him.

Rob grabbed the oars and started rowing, jolting the boat forward.

'You may not be interested in the finer points of fly fishing, Rob,' said Euan, 'but you'll not catch fish if you don't know what you're doing.'

'And you're the local expert are you?' said Rob.

Euan flipped open his fishing box. Trays of brightly coloured artificial flies opened out in front of us. 'You can't just use any old fly,' he said. 'Depends on time of year, weather and all that.' He picked up a large black fly and examined it lovingly. The hook glistened under the fan of black feathers. 'This here is a Bristol Black. It's a hopper. The trout thinks it's a juicy land insect like a grasshopper blown across on the water. Now this one is perfect for a warm windy day in late summer. If there's any trout out there, this'll catch it.'

I stretched out on one of the seats and stared at the sky, listening to the dull clunk of oars in the rowlocks and gurgle of water under the boat.

'I was a bit scared of Iona, you know,' said Rob.

I watched the puffy clouds sail overhead. 'She could be a bit fierce at times,' I said. I couldn't help a smile.

I looked across at Rob. 'She could stalk up on red deer,' I said, 'get to within an arm's length. Remember when she caught a trout in her hands that day we first saw her?'

Rob stowed the oars and let the little boat drift in the breeze. He trailed his hand in the water and stared at his broken reflection.

'Tickling trout is clever all right,' said Euan. 'But *this*, Callum,' he said standing up in the boat, '*this* is pure art.' He flicked his rod and cast the fly out across the water. It sailed through the air and landed with a distant plop.

Rob stretched out on the other seat and closed his eyes.

Sky Hawk

'What d'you reckon, Callum? Will it be fish fingers and chips for tea?'

'Laugh all you like,' said Euan, his back to us. 'I'll have a nice fat trout for mine.'

We drifted slowly across the loch into early evening. The hot peaty air buzzed with a billion insects. Somewhere out on the pastures, a curlew called out and above me swallows and swifts swooped through the air.

'Is there any more food?' said Rob rummaging in my rucksack.

'I think you've eaten most of it,' I said.

'I'm starving,' said Rob. 'Caught any fish yet, Euan?'

Euan just glowered at him.

'Maybe you're not casting right,' said Rob. 'D'you want me to have a go?'

'The day I need a casting lesson from you, I'll give up fishing,' snapped Euan.

I watched the end of Euan's rod flick backwards and upwards before he cast the fly across the water. High in the sky above us, the broad barred wings of an osprey sailed into view. It circled, scanning the loch below. It was hunting. It was Iris's mate looking for fish for its chick.

Rob and Euan were still arguing with each other.

'Maybe you're using the wrong type of rod?' said Rob.

'This is the best rod money can buy. Carbon fibre it is,' said Euan.

The osprey beat its wings in a hover motion. It was preparing to dive. I'd seen this before, but each time filled me with the same thrill.

'Maybe you're using the wrong fly,' suggested Rob.

'Ah, shut your face, Rob,' snapped Euan. 'There's no trout in this loch. I've got more chance of catching a goldfish.' He flicked the end of his rod making the fly jerk across the water.

The osprey dived. Wings closed. Head forward. Talons out.

A blur through the sky, it plunged into the water near Euan's Bristol Hopper. Water sprayed into the air. I expected the osprey to fly straight out, but it beat its wings a couple of times and just sat there in the water, bobbing about and staring at us.

'What the bloody hell is that?' spluttered Rob.

'Osprey!' said Euan.

It shook its head and beat its wings, rising upwards. It struggled, flapping hard, its talons trailing deep in the water. It finally broke the surface not far from our boat and shook itself, scattering a rainbow in the diamond drops of water. Beneath the osprey, grasped in its talons, was one of the biggest trout I had ever seen. It was so close I could see the bright red of the gills flap open and shut.

Rob almost fell out of the boat laughing so much. But Euan just sat there, open mouthed. For the first time in his life he was utterly speechless.

Euan Douglas had been out-fished.

CHAPTER 21

'Osprey!' said Euan, flopping down in the boat. He watched the osprey carry the trout back to the eyrie where the young osprey pulled it from him. 'You've got osprey nesting on your farm. Why didn't you tell us?'

I stared at the ripples of the boat's wake. 'They're rare,' I mumbled, 'protected.'

'And you thought we'd go and blab to everyone,' said Euan. He looked hurt now, angry. 'You didn't think you could trust us?'

I grabbed the oars and pulled hard on them. 'It wasn't like that,' I said.

'Did *she* know?' asked Rob.

I nodded. 'Iona found them. She saved them . . . well, Iris that is.'

'*Iris?*' said Rob with a laugh.

'Yes, Iris,' I snapped. 'Why d'you have to make a stupid bloody joke out of everything?' I rowed the boat across the loch, the oars slapping in the water. The boat crunched on the gritty shore and I jumped out and looped the rope over a tree stump. 'I promised Iona I'd look after Iris. And I will. I'll do it.'

I stormed off along the path. Rob and Euan had to run to catch up with me.

Rob grabbed me by the arm. 'I'm sorry, all right?'

I turned on him angrily. 'You said I was a complete loser, remember?'

'I was mad at you. You couldn't be bothered with us any more.'

'It was the ospreys,' I said. 'I . . . ' My voice trailed off and I sank onto a damp mossy stone.

Euan leaned against a tree. 'So where's she now? Where's Iris?'

'Gone,' I said. 'She's heading south for the winter.'

'So that's it, is it?' said Euan. 'You'll have to wait till next year?'

I sat there picking the bits of moss and rolling them between my fingers.

'No,' I said.

Neither Rob nor Euan said a word.

I flicked the moss to the ground. 'I can follow her. She's got a radio transmitter on her back. I'll see her journey all the way to Africa and back.'

'You're kidding me?' said Rob. He was wide-eyed.

'No,' I said. 'Iona and me, we helped fit the transmitter.'

'Now *that* is cool,' whistled Rob. 'How do you track her?'

'On my computer,' I said.

'Can you show us?' said Rob.

I shrugged my shoulders.

Euan gave me a hard stare. 'For God's sake, Callum, we're your mates. Can't you trust us?'

I looked across at them. Dad was right. They were my friends, and right now, I needed them.

'Of course I trust you,' I said.

'Come on, then,' said Rob picking up my rucksack. 'I can't wait to see this.'

Back in my bedroom, Euan and Rob leaned over my shoulder as I switched on the computer.

'Iris is in southern France,' I said. 'She'll have to fly over the Pyrenees soon.'

'The what?' said Rob.

Sky Hawk

'Pyrenees,' said Euan, 'the mountains between France and Spain.'

I showed them how to tap in Iris's code so we could find her position and plot it on the maps of Google Earth.

'Look,' I said. 'That's where she was an hour ago.'

```
              25th August
               19.00 GMT
        Lourdes, South of France
    43°05'08.94" N   0°05'43.43" W
             Speed: 26 km/h
           Altitude: 1.18km
           Direction: South
     Total distance: 1771.86km
```

Rob took over the computer. 'Amazing,' he said. 'You can see everything she flies over. And look at this.' He clicked on tiny photo icons scattered over the maps. 'There are even photos of the places. Just look at these mountains, they're massive!'

I pulled out my diary and wrote the coordinates inside.

'What's that?' asked Euan.

'A diary,' I said. 'I plot her journey in it too.'

'Can I look?' asked Euan.

I passed it over and he slowly flicked through all the

pages. I'd stuck in some of Iona's paintings and sketches.

'These are good drawings,' said Euan.

I nodded. 'Iona did them.'

'Can I draw something?' he said.

I passed Euan a pencil and let him sketch a picture at the bottom of the page. He held up the finished drawing and showed me. It wasn't as good as Iona's, but I liked it all the same.

It was three boys in a boat on the loch, and an osprey catching a huge brown trout from the water.

Chapter 22

27th August
07.48 GMT
Pyrenees, Spain
42°45′28.29″ N   0°21′41.68″ W
Speed: 68.8 km/h
Altitude: 3.21km
Direction: South
Total distance: 1865.23 km

'Iris has left France,' I said at breakfast. 'She's over the Pyrenees right now. I've just had a reading.'

'Very nice,' said Dad, pouring himself a cup of tea. 'I hope she's stocked up on croissants for the journey.'

'Dad, that's not even funny.'

Mum pushed a bowl of porridge under my nose.

'She's flying really high,' I said, 'at over three thousand

metres. She's going some too. She's flying at nearly seventy kilometres an hour. That's some tail wind behind her.'

'Aye, and you'll need more than a tail wind to get you to school on time,' said Mum tapping the bowl with her spoon. 'First day back, you can't be late. Dad'll have to give you a lift.'

Rob, Euan, and I were all in the top class now. One more year and we'd leave the village school for the secondary school twenty miles away by bus. Dad drove me to school and dropped me at the school gates.

The bell was ringing so I hurried inside to our new classroom.

Rob flung his bag on the desk next to me. 'A whole year of Mrs Wicklow,' he groaned.

'She taught my dad when he was here,' said Euan flopping in a chair.

'She's ancient,' said Rob.

Euan nodded. 'My dad swears she's got mountain troll blood in her.'

I gave Euan a nudge as Mrs Wicklow strode through the door.

'Good morning, class,' she bellowed.

The class fell silent as she turned to glare at the three of us, before turning to write on the board.

Sky Hawk

'You'll be pleased to know we're starting the term with a project on castles and fortified towns,' she said. 'We'll be looking at why they were built and what life was like when people lived there. Work in groups. Find out as much as you can and present a project to the class.'

Rob, Euan, and I sat down at a spare computer and searched under 'castles'.

'How about Edinburgh Castle, that's a good one,' said Euan.

'Nearly everyone did that last year,' said Mrs Wicklow. 'I want something different.'

Euan muttered under his breath as Mrs Wicklow left the room.

Rob was spinning in his chair next to us. I searched through all the kids' web pages, but nothing really grabbed me. All I could think about was where Iris was right now. What could she see? Had she made it over the Pyrenees?

'Come on, Rob,' I said. 'Don't expect us to do all the work.'

Rob whizzed over and bashed his chair into mine.

'OK, budge up,' he said.

He tapped in Iris's code.

'Not here, Rob,' I hissed. 'We don't want anyone to see.'

'Come on,' said Rob. 'Troll-face isn't here.'

The computer took ages initializing into Google Earth. The clock timer spun over and over.

'Chair race!' announced Rob. 'You up for it?'

It was our thing. We'd race each other by spinning the swivel chairs round and round from the bottom seat position to the top and back down again.

'Three . . . two . . . one . . . GO,' said Rob.

And we were off. Spinning like crazy. I kept my arms and legs tucked in. Round and round and round we spun. Rob and Euan were whirling blurs beside me.

My seat hit the bottom position with a clunk. 'I won,' I yelled. Euan came seconds in behind me, but he was looking beyond me, his face pale.

'Callum McGregor!'

I turned and my blood froze.

Mrs Wicklow was standing behind me, hands on hips. She turned to the class. 'Well, it seems Mr McGregor and his friends have time enough to play games.'

Everyone was staring at us. The class was silent.

'Let's see what these three have found for their research,' said Mrs Wicklow taking a step towards the computer.

Rob reached over and hammered a few keys on the keyboard. I wanted to pull the socket from the wall. In a few moments, Iris's secret would be there for all to see.

Sky Hawk

'Come on now,' snapped Mrs Wicklow.

Rob had time to press one more key. Mrs Wicklow sat down and stared at the screen. She raised her eyebrows and looked at me. 'I didn't know you had an interest in Northern Spain; the Pyrenees, to be precise.'

I looked at Euan but there was nothing to be done.

Mrs Wicklow turned the screen to the class. 'Well done to Callum, Rob, and Euan,' she said.

I looked at the screen. It didn't show Iris or the route she'd taken over the mountains. Instead there was an article on the most amazing castle I had ever seen. It had turrets and high walls and was perched on the very edge of high mountains, like the edge of the world itself.

'Castillo de Loarre,' said Rob in a forced Spanish accent, 'high in the Pyrenees.'

Mrs Wicklow raised her eyebrows. 'Good work, boys,' she said. 'Keep it up.'

When she had moved across the class I turned to Rob. 'How did you find that one?'

Rob laughed. 'Sheer luck,' he said. 'I clicked on the nearest photo to Iris's position, just to take the attention away from her. I couldn't believe it when it showed this castle. I clicked on the link and here it is.'

I looked closer at the screen. 'Amazing, isn't it,' I said.

'To think she has flown over this very castle less than an hour ago. Maybe it's one of her landmarks.'

'Forget that,' said Rob running his hand through his hair. 'That bird just saved our skin.'

27th August
11.15 GMT
Loarre, Northern Spain
42°18′49.42″ N   0°37′29.39″ W
Speed: 28.6 km/h
Altitude: 1.42km
Direction: South
Total distance: 1908.34 km

CHAPTER 23

We followed Iris's journey every day. It took her three days to reach the south of Spain. She stayed near a reservoir there for nearly a week before heading off across the Straits of Gibraltar. I rang Hamish to say she had left for Africa. Hamish told me he'd been to Gibraltar before and seen loads of different migrating birds waiting for the right conditions to cross the stretch of water. He said it was like an airport lounge for different birds, squabbling for space until the right wind direction or clear skies carried them over the sea.

But it was the desert that worried me. On the map the huge expanse of the Sahara Desert stretched across Northern Africa. Pictures showed endless seas of sand-dunes. I read about rocks so hot you could fry an egg, and sandstorms so fierce, they could tear your skin off. It was hard to believe that Iris would fly over this furnace of land, with no water to drink or fish from.

And then my worst fear happened.

There was no signal from Iris.

I rang Hamish.

'Maybe she's sheltering in rocks,' he said. 'If the solar battery loses power in the dark it won't transmit the signal.'

'But it's the middle of the day,' I said. 'She should be flying. There's enough sun out there. It's the Sahara.'

'I know,' said Hamish with a sigh. 'We'll just have to wait. It's all we can do.'

I couldn't sleep much that night. I woke early and tapped in Iris's code on the computer.

11th September
NO SIGNAL

'I've lost her, Dad,' I said. 'There was no signal yesterday. She went too far east into the Sahara.'

Dad flicked the edge of my bedroom curtain. It was still dark outside and sleet skittered against the windows. 'I need help with the sheep, Cal. We've got to bring them down from the hills.'

'She's one hundred and seventy-eight kilometres from water.'

'There's a couple of lame ewes I want to look at.'

'It's not yet dawn in the Sahara. Maybe when the sun hits the solar panel on her transmitter, we'll find her again.'

Dad looked at me. I didn't think he'd been listening to a word I said, but he had.

'Cal,' he said, 'I want Iris to be safe too, but it's not going to make any difference if you sit all day with your face pressed to that computer screen. She's a wild bird, in a harsh environment. You know that. There's nothing you can do to help her out there, she's on her own.'

'But she's a fighter, Dad. Isn't she?' I looked at the screen, at the exact point of her last signal. Every day of her journey, I'd zoomed in on Google Earth to her location. I'd panned over the landscape she was flying over. It was as if I was with her. It was as if I was flying right beside her all the way.

'Come on, Cal,' Dad said. 'Have your breakfast and help me with the sheep. Maybe we can go up to the osprey nest later and fix it for storm damage. There's going to be high winds tonight. Let's make sure the nest is there for her next spring. It's all we can do.'

I turned to switch the computer off, but before I could press the keys, a small orange dot flashed on the screen, a small orange dot that could only mean one thing. 'She's back, Dad,' I yelled. 'There's a signal. There, in the desert. It's her signal.'

Dad peered at the screen and ran his hands through my hair. 'Aye,' he smiled. 'Maybe she's dipping her toes in a green oasis right now, a long cool drink by her side.'

'Dad!' I gave him a shove, but I couldn't take the grin off my face.

```
        11th September
         5.30 GMT
        Sahara Desert
31°30'08.84" N    0°41'37.21" E
         Speed: 0 km/h
   Total distance: 3812.02 km
```

Iris opened her eyes and ruffled her feathers. A pale orange dawn was spreading across the horizon. There were no landmarks to be seen, no green-lined oasis or bright strip of river. There were only the pale golden dunes rolling endlessly into the distance.

The sandstorm had raged all day and all night. It had blown Iris far into the desert where she found shelter beneath an outcrop of rock. Gritty sand had worked its way into her mouth and nostrils and rubbed on the soft skin beneath the downy feathers. One foot was swollen and ached where the old cut lay open, and her long flight feathers were dry and brittle from the heat. She started preening them, oiling them so the barbs on each were smooth and sealed again.

As the sun flared into the sky, Iris launched herself up into the rising spirals of air. All day she drifted southwards and westwards. The desert sun burned into her back and the midday sand glared bright in her eyes. As the sun curved down towards the horizon, Iris sank down with it through the cooling layers of air.

Below, a trail of camels and people trudged over the high

dune ridges, their long dark shadows pressed against the golden sand. A child riding high on one of the camels pointed to her as she passed. Deep within Iris, the memories of the distant cold-lands flowed through her, memories of a child watching, of rich fishing grounds and deep waters. They lifted her and carried her higher. And in the fading light a green smudge of trees and scrubland appeared, and beyond that, at last a strip of sunset reflected in the curves of a wide flowing river.

Chapter 24

Iplotted Iris's journey in my diary over the following weeks and downloaded photos of some of the places she had flown across. One was the bizarre Richat Structure in Mauritania, a pattern of huge circles in the desert that NASA scientists could see from space. She flew across towns with strange names such as Ksar el Barka and Boutilimit. There were photos of whole villages gradually being swallowed up by huge sand-dunes and photos of camel trains heading into pale desert dawns.

Iris's flight took her south and west into Senegal and on to The Gambia. Her long migration came to an end along the banks of the River Gambia, not far from its opening to the sea. I looked at photos of the area. Dense green mangrove swamps and palms came down to the water's edge. Crocodiles slept on domed mud banks at low tide. Fishermen mended nets alongside brightly painted boats.

23rd September
08.00
Mangrove swamp, The Gambia
13°16'28.05" N   16°28'58.14" W
Speed: 0 km/h
Total distance: 6121.23 km

It was so different from the lochs and mountains of Scotland. And it had only taken her thirty-nine days to travel all the way. Hamish said some ospreys they had tracked made the flight in much less time.

Each day after that, Iris's signals came from the same area. Her flight pattern made zigzags across a small river inlet where she fished, to roost trees in the riverbanks. She seemed settled and I didn't check her position so often. I would have to wait until March before she started her migration north to Scotland again.

I sat down at the computer in my bedroom to check on her position. I hadn't logged on for a couple of days. I turned on the computer, ready to tap in Iris's code.

A stone pinged against my bedroom window.

I opened the window to see Rob and Euan in the yard below on their bikes.

Sky Hawk

'Are you coming, Callum? We're going up the top trails.'

I looked up at the hills. The trees blazed red and gold in the October sunshine. It was a perfect day.

'Coming,' I yelled. Iris would have to wait. I logged off and grabbed my fleece.

Rob was wearing a bright new helmet, black with silver stripes.

'It's a present from my mum,' said Rob. 'She got called in by Troll-face. I thought I was in trouble, but Troll-face just wanted tell her how well I was doing. "An enthusiastic approach to geography," she said.'

'Can't think why,' said Euan with a grin.

We headed out around the back of the farm. Even Rob had to push his bike up the hill. We pushed and pulled our bikes up the rutted dry stream beds and sheep tracks. When we reached the top we flopped down in the heather.

'It's still there then,' said Euan.

He was looking across to the osprey eyrie on the island. There had been some stormy nights since the ospreys left.

'Dad and Hamish went up and fixed it to the top,' I said.

'Why d'you reckon they migrate?' said Rob. 'I mean, why bother? Why not stay here?'

'Too cold in the winter probably,' I said.

'So why not stay in Africa,' said Rob, 'where it's hot and there's always fish?'

I shrugged my shoulders. 'Maybe their nests are safer here. I mean it's not as if we have monkeys or snakes and things to eat the eggs or young birds.'

'Some people steal them,' said Euan.

'Bunch of weirdoes,' I said. 'That's what Hamish calls them.'

'Come on,' said Rob.

We followed him along the top trail across the ridge of the hill. It was smooth riding, with a few gullies to whizz down and up the other side. The sky was summer-sky blue, reflected in the loch below.

'Hey, down here,' said Rob. He turned his bike down a steep track through the pine forest. 'Slalom practice!'

We followed Rob's trail in and out of the trees. The branches were so low I had to duck right down not to be knocked off. We shot out of the dark pines into an open bit of forest Dad had cleared and replanted with native trees. We whizzed past the young saplings fenced off from deer and down into the woods of oak and wild cherry that lined the loch.

Rob skidded to a stop in a ring of white boulders. I hadn't realized we'd come so near to the tree-house. It was only yards away.

Sky Hawk

'What is this place?' said Rob. 'We've never been here before.'

Euan was off his bike and walking round the circle of stones.

'It's like they were placed here,' he said.

'Let's go,' I said.

'We've only just got here,' said Rob. He scrambled up on the top of one boulder. A shaft of sunlight broke through on his face. 'Perfect,' he said.

He lay back against the stone and closed his eyes. If he looked up now, he would see the tree-house right above him. I didn't want to tell them about it, not yet. I couldn't face going back up there. I pushed my bike down towards the track by the loch and waited.

'What's up with you, Cal?' shouted Euan.

'I'm starving,' I said. 'Let's see if Mum'll give us some food.'

Rob jumped down to join us and we cycled slowly along the track. Autumn leaves, blood red, floated on the dark waters of the loch and clogged together round the edges of the shore.

'Who's that?' said Euan.

A figure in blue shirt and jeans stood at the far end of the loch.

'That's Hamish,' I said. 'The wildlife officer I was telling you about.'

I pushed my way in front of Rob and cycled ahead of the others.

'Hi, Hamish,' I said.

Rob and Euan pulled up beside us on their bikes.

'This is Rob,' I said, 'and Euan.'

Hamish nodded at them, but he didn't have his usual cheery smile.

'It doesn't look good, does it?' he said.

'What?' I didn't know what he was talking about.

'Iris,' he said. 'Haven't you noticed?'

'I haven't checked on her for a day or two,' I said.

Hamish shook his head. 'She's not moved position for three days. Her signal is coming from a mangrove swamp. She hasn't made any flights to fish or find new roost sites. It doesn't look good.'

I kicked the ground. 'I should have checked on her,' I said.

'It's not like you can do anything,' said Rob.

'I made a promise,' I said. 'I promised Iona I would look after Iris.'

'Rob's right,' said Hamish. He put his hand on my shoulder. 'There's nothing you can do. Ospreys face loads of dangers. It's only now we're tracking them, we know how many survive the long migration.'

I shook off Hamish. 'I made a promise,' I said.

'Callum . . .' said Hamish.

'I'll find a way,' I yelled. I pushed off down the rutted track along the loch, but all I could see ahead of me was a knotted maze of waterways reaching into dense green mangrove swamp.

CHAPTER 25

'Absolutely not.'

'But *why* not?' I said.

Mum thumped the casserole down on the table. 'For a start, we can't afford it. Then you've got to have loads of jabs and tablets for malaria weeks before you even think of going there. And you're eleven, for goodness' sake. The answer's, "no", Callum. You're not going to The Gambia, final.'

I stood up. 'I'm not hungry,' I said.

'Sit down, Callum,' said Dad. He dished a pile of potatoes on my plate. 'Even if we could get out there, what then? We don't know anything about the place. How would we find her in a mangrove forest? It would be like looking for a needle in a haystack.'

Sky Hawk

'So that's it, is it?' I shouted. 'Give up, just like that?'

'Yes, Callum,' said Dad. 'That's exactly what we do. We can't do anything from here. She's a wild bird. You know that.'

I slammed my knife and fork down and stormed up to my room. I flicked the computer on and looked for Iris's signal. It hadn't moved for three days. How could I have not noticed? I should have checked on her. I should have checked. I zoomed in as far as I could get. I could almost see the individual trees. Iris was in there somewhere. I wanted to reach in through the computer and pick her up.

Maybe I could somehow get to The Gambia myself. I looked up tourist information on the web. There were masses of hotels along the coast and smaller camps and eco-lodges inland along the river. They all had addresses and websites.

Of course, that was it!

I needed to contact someone in The Gambia to look for Iris.

I wrote email after email to hotels, eco-lodges, companies specializing in bird watching trips. I emailed a church group, a hospital. I even tried to email the Gambian government.

Now all I could do was to wait.

Dad came up to my room with my supper.

'Sorry,' he said. He placed the plate on the desk beside

me. 'It's not your fault, you know.'

I sighed. 'I should have checked on her.'

Dad put his arms around my shoulders. 'It's not your fault Iona died.'

I just stared into the deep, deep blue of the computer screen.

CHAPTER 26

Rob and Euan came home with me after school the next day.

'Have you had any replies?' said Euan.

I shook my head. 'No, only two emails which bounced back unable to connect, and another advertising cheap flights and hotels.'

Rob sat down at my desk. 'Come on then,' he said. 'Let's see if anyone else has replied.' He switched on my computer.

Euan and I leaned over his shoulder. The computer took an age to warm up.

Rob flicked onto my emails.

Please let there be an email, please, I thought.

Rob pressed the send/receive icon.

I couldn't take my eyes off the screen.

Receiving messages
One message received.

From: Jeneba Kah
Sent: 8th October 15:30 GMT

Subject: Hello Callum

Hello Callum.
My name is Jeneba Kah. Doctor Jawara opened your
email and asked me to write to you. He said it would be
good for my English. I think maybe this is an excuse and
Dr Jawara is hoping for a little rest from my questions.
Maybe one day I will be a great doctor like him and
someone will ask me the questions. But this is good,
because I have not had a go on a computer before.
I like the photo of your bird.

I am sorry, I have not seen her. I am in hospital and
too far from the river. But I have seen birds like her fish
in the river near my village. We call them kulanjango.
They like to fish when the river tide is far in, or far out.
My father is a fisherman and he is always happy to see
the kulanjango, or osprey as you call them, come home.
They bring him luck to catch many fish. When my father
and brother come to visit me tomorrow, I will ask them to
search for her.

Scotland is very far away. I have just looked on a map.
From Jeneba aged 10

Are you a girl or a boy? I am a girl.

Rob slammed his hands on the desk. 'Result!' he shouted.

Euan stared at the screen. 'You've done it,' he said.
'You've actually done it.'

I couldn't stop grinning. 'I can't believe it,' I said. 'There's really someone out there who can help us. We'll find Iris now. I know we will.'

'Write back then,' said Rob.

'What, now?' I said. 'To her? To Jeneba?'

Rob nodded. 'Well, who d'you think?'

My hands hovered over the computer keys. I looked up at Euan. 'What shall I say?'

Euan rolled his eyes. 'Just say, thanks very much and tell us when you find Iris.'

'OK,' I said, 'OK.' I took a deep breath, and started typing . . .

From: Callum
Sent: 8th October 16:43 GMT

Subject: Looking for Iris

Hello Jeneba,
Thanks very much and please tell me if you find Iris.
Callum (boy 11)

'There,' I said. 'it's a bit short.'

Rob sat back in the chair. 'It's fine,' he said. 'Just send it off. No good staring at it.'

I pressed the 'send' icon and watched the message

disappear. 'All we can do now is wait,' I said.

I looked for Iris's position after supper, but she had completely disappeared from the screen.

It's nearly night-time, I told myself. The solar battery isn't charged, it can't give out its signal. But a deeper fear stirred uneasily within me. I had to believe in tomorrow. I had to believe Iris was still alive.

CHAPTER 27

The next day, I woke up with a sore throat. It was a Saturday, cold and grey. Dad had gone off early to market, and Graham was away for the weekend with friends. Mum wrapped me in a duvet and put me in front of the TV. I hardly moved all day except to check my emails.

I had one reply from a birding holiday company who said they didn't go to that part of The Gambia.

But still nothing from Jeneba.

I watched the hands of the grandfather clock creep slowly round and round. The afternoon light outside faded into darkness. The TV blared on: cartoons, football, quiz programmes and golf. Dad came home with Chinese take-away and bottles of Coke.

'Look who's here,' said Dad.

Hamish came in and sat next to me on the sofa. 'I heard about your email,' he said. 'It's amazing. You've actually made contact with someone who can look for Iris.'

I shrugged my shoulders. 'Seems like a long shot,' I said. 'I haven't heard back from the Gambian girl today.'

Mum came in with bowls of chicken chow mein and put them on the small table by the TV.

'You said you'd find a way,' said Hamish.

'I've left it too late,' I said.

'You don't know that,' said Dad. 'You've got this far, when everyone else was prepared to give up.'

'Get that down in writing,' laughed Mum. 'Dad never admits to being wrong.'

'I mean it,' said Dad. 'It just shows you, doesn't it? What you can do when you really want something.'

Hamish nodded and picked up a bowl and a pair of chopsticks. I wasn't that hungry, so I left them watching a game show and dragged my duvet up the stairs.

I turned on my computer and waited.

It wasn't until bedtime that another email from Jeneba came through.

Sky Hawk

From: Jeneba Kah
Sent: 9th October 21:00 GMT

Subject: Looking for Iris

Hello Callum,
No news, I'm sorry.

My father and brother went fishing today and have been
looking for Iris. I wish I could have gone with them, but I
cannot. An American student doctor called Max went with
them. He used his GPS to try and find her. Max said they
went to the place where Iris's last signal came from, but she
wasn't there.

The kulanjango are very important to the fishermen. My
father says he will visit the marabout. He is our village wise
man. The marabout is blind, but he sees things other people
cannot see. Maybe he can help find Iris.
My father did not catch any fish today.

I hope to bring you good news tomorrow.

Jeneba.

I phoned Hamish on his mobile. I told him they didn't
find Iris at the place of her last signal and now her signal had
disappeared. I could almost hear Hamish's disappointment
on the phone. He said maybe the harness holding the
transmitter had broken and come off. They were designed
to break eventually. Maybe she was fine and still flying
around.

But I knew that she could as easily be in the belly of a crocodile somewhere.

It was now five days since Iris had stopped moving. I couldn't help thinking something was wrong. If she was alive, she'd be weak with hunger by now. We were running out of time.

Chapter 28

From: Jeneba Kah
Sent: 10th October 06.30 GMT

Subject: Looking for Iris

Hello Callum,
I have just seen Max on his ward round this morning.
He went with my father and the villagers and visited the
marabout last night. The marabout lives in a small hut
outside our village between the peanut fields and the
mangroves. Max said the marabout burned wet leaves
on a small fire and filled his hut with a sweet smoke that
smelled of flowers after the rains. He said the marabout
spread his arms wide like wings, and called to the bird
spirit. The smoke from his fire drifted out from the hut like
a great white bird and flew out over the forest. Max said
he had never seen anything like it before. I don't think
they have marabouts in America.

Today the marabout is going in my father's boat to find
Iris. He told the people from my village that he has seen

this bird in his dreams. He says it carries the future of the village on its wings. Everyone from the village is going to look for Iris too.

The marabout is never wrong.

Max is joining them. He is taking his camera to show me the pictures when they return.

Dr Jawara is waiting to use his computer now, so I will write you later with news of Iris.

Your friend,

Jeneba.

I read the email to Mum and Dad on the way to church.

'Sounds a bit voodoo to me,' said Dad. 'You know, I mean witch doctors and that stuff.'

'Maybe there is a bird spirit,' I said.

'It's a bit far-fetched,' said Mum.

'So is church, when you think about it,' I said. 'We're meant to believe in the Holy Spirit and loads of miracles and things.'

'So you should,' said Mum.

Dad pulled up opposite the churchyard. 'Come on,' he said. 'Let's see what marabout Parsons has got to tell us this week.'

Mum gave Dad a hard stare. I laughed and followed them under the yew and up the path into the little church.

Sky Hawk

Reverend Parsons gave his sermon from his wooden pulpit. The top was carved into an eagle with outspread wings. Maybe there was a bird spirit. Maybe the marabout could see Iris somehow, and feel her. I closed my eyes and tried to imagine her in the mangrove forest. I thought of the last signal I had written in my diary. I tried to think what could have happened to her, where she could be, right now.

Iris pressed herself against the smooth mangrove bark. The incoming tide swirled around the tangled roots and small fish darted in and out of the shadows. Pain throbbed through her body from the old wound on her foot. It was red and swollen and oozed thick pus and streaks of blood. Six nights had passed since she had caught any fish.

Below, a snake swam through the green waters, its head above the surface trailing a sinuous wake behind. Its tongue flickered in the air, smelling, feeling for prey. It began to slide towards Iris. She flapped hard and lifted up into the warm still air, above the mangroves and green river. The tide rippled in gentle eddies around domed mud banks where crocodiles slumbered in the heat. Insects buzzed in the air and a fisherman drifted slowly in his boat. Only the flicker of fish beneath the water broke the stillness.

Iris dived. She dropped down, wings folded, talons outstretched. The mirrored flat surface rushed to meet her. A flash of silver shot deep, but she struck and her good foot grasped fish.

She beat upwards from the river, up into a black shadow of killing talons and beak.

Iris twisted away. The fish-eagle banked, close on her tail, chasing her across open water. She could hear the whistle of its wings and the downward rush of air. She let the fish fall. The eagle grasped it in its talons and soared on with its stolen catch.

Iris flew back into the mangroves to an old dead tree on the banks of a creek. Her body ached, and fever sapped her strength. She pushed herself through rotting bark into the hollowed trunk, and leaned against the cool damp wood. She closed her eyes, and fell through endless darkness, deeper and deeper into a dreamless and fevered sleep.

Chapter 29

I couldn't concentrate on anything all day. I'd checked on my emails after church, but there was nothing. There was still no signal from Iris either.

'You need to get some fresh air,' said Mum. 'It'll make your sore throat better.'

'You can bring in the sheep from the bottom field,' said Dad. 'I need to check on those lame ones again.'

I unclipped Kip, our young sheep dog. He was a bit fresh and keen when Dad first got him. Some friends with young children had visited once, and Kip had rounded them all up into one of the barns. But he mostly rounded up the sheep now, or the chickens to get them in the chicken shed.

Kip and I headed down the valley towards the village. The ground was boggy underfoot. Deep tyre tracks had ground into the mud in the gateways. I splashed through the puddles, the water almost coming over the top of my boots.

Kip was already ahead of me racing towards the sheep at the far end of the field. Dad usually took him out with Elsie the old dog so he could learn from her. I whistled to Kip but the wind was against me. He raced in too fast and the sheep scattered. Then he didn't know which way to run. I whistled again and this time he heard. I sent him around the back of the sheep and made him lie down. The sheep calmed and bunched themselves together again. Then I whistled for him to bring them on slowly. He was good at it too, going one way then the other, moving them forward. He trotted swiftly, his belly low. His eyes never left the sheep. Dad said that it was an old hunting instinct of wolves that had been bred into Border collies. It always amazed me to think of behaviour so hardwired into their system that it was actually part of them, inseparable. Like the ospreys and their migration. It made me think what could be buried deep inside me.

I let Kip drive the sheep past me and away up the hill to the farmyard. A cold wind blew in my face all the way back. The clouds were low and grey, trailing wisps across the tops of the hills. Dad and Graham were waiting for the sheep in the yard. I chained Kip back into his kennel and added more straw and a handful of dog biscuits and sneaked back into the kitchen.

'I've made tablet,' said Mum.

The sweet crumbly fudge was my favourite. I grabbed a few pieces and headed up to my bedroom.

This morning I'd believed that the marabout would find Iris. But now it did seem a bit far-fetched. Mum was probably right. How could they possibly find her in miles and miles of mangrove forest? She could be anywhere.

I switched on my computer to look at my emails.

There was another one from Jeneba, with an attachment.

I hardly dared open it. If it was bad news, it would be too hard to take.

I clicked on the email. There was no message, just one attachment.

I held my breath.

And opened it.

Iris was staring right at me from the screen with her brilliant yellow eyes. A large pair of dark brown hands was folded round her body. Her feathers were tatty and dull, and one leg hung limply beneath her. But it was definitely Iris.

She was alive.

CHAPTER 30

'Amazing,' said Euan. 'To think they've actually found her.' He sat down at my computer after school the next day to look at the photograph of Iris.

'You've got another email,' said Rob, 'and another picture.'

From: Jeneba Kah
Sent: 11th October 15.30 GMT

Subject: Iris

Hello Callum,
I hope you got the photo yesterday. Max took it with his camera. It made the computer crash when I tried to send it and Dr Jawara was not very happy. But Max has fixed the computer and I am allowed to use it again.

159

Yesterday was an exciting day. All the villagers went out on boats with my father and the marabout. I wish I could have been there too. Max showed me the photos. He said it was like a big party. The marabout told them to look in dense forest and rotting trees. He said she was not far from the place my father and Max were looking yesterday.

Everyone was looking for Iris all afternoon. My brother found her in a hollow rotten tree.

The fishermen caught a lot of fish yesterday. Iris has brought them good luck.

Max is looking after Iris in a shed next to his apartment. She is very weak. He has been feeding her mashed fish through a tube into her stomach because she is too sick to feed herself. There is an old cut on her foot which has become infected so Max is giving her antibiotics.

Max wanted to bring Iris into the ward to show me, but Mama Binta got real cross at him. She said she didn't want no 'fishing chicken' in her ward. All birds are chickens to Mama Binta. Last week three goats got into the hospital and chewed up some blankets. Mama Binta got so mad with those old goats I think she almost put them in the stew pot.

Mama Binta is the head nurse here. She sees everything. If things aren't clean and spotless, she is like a crocodile with a sore tooth. Even the doctors are afraid of her.

She says I make a nuisance of myself asking all my questions and keeping the other children in the ward awake. That's why she carries me to Doctor Jawara's office to write to you.

I can hear Mama Binta coming to fetch me, so I must go now. I have attached another photo that Max has taken.

I will write you when I can about Iris.

Your friend, Jeneba.

Sky Hawk

I clicked on the attachment, wanting to see Iris again, as if I needed more proof she was alive. But it wasn't Iris. It was a photo of a girl with dark brown skin and one of the biggest smiles I have ever seen.

It was Jeneba.

'That's really her?' said Euan pushing Rob's head out of the way.

'I guess so,' I said.

We all stared at the photo. Jeneba was sitting up in a hospital bed with two huge plaster casts around her legs. Another child, much younger, was asleep beside her in the same bed. The bed looked old, like something out of an antique shop. Red rust showed through the white blistered paint. In the background was a large nurse dressed in blue uniform leaning over another bed. Three small children lay in that bed. One boy looked so small, so skinny. He was attached to a big bag of clear liquid above his head by a long plastic tube that went into his arm. He looked fast asleep, dead almost. Beyond the rows of beds was an open door leading into bright sunlight.

'Bit crowded in there,' said Rob. 'Don't they have enough beds?'

'Same as here in Scotland,' said Euan. 'My nan had her operation cancelled three times because there weren't enough beds.'

Rob pulled a face. 'Uggh! Imagine having to share a bed with your nan.'

Euan shuddered. 'I think I'd rather die.'

I pushed Euan away to get a better look at the photo of Jeneba. 'What d'you think happened to her legs?' I said.

Euan shrugged his shoulders.

'Crocodile,' said Rob.

'What?'

'I bet she's been chomped by a crocodile,' said Rob. He snapped his hands together. 'It happens all the time out there. I saw it on TV. One minute she'll have been paddling in the river fetching water, next minute . . . chomp.'

'You don't know that,' I said.

'I bet you anything it was a crocodile,' he said. He leaned over and started writing a message on the computer.

Sky Hawk

From: Callum, Rob and Euan
Sent: 11th October 18.50 GMT

Subject: Crocodile

Hi Jeneba,
I'm Rob, one of Callum's friends.

Did your legs get chomped by a crocodile? I saw a TV
programme where a man escaped from a crocodile by
poking it in the eye with a stick. How did you do it?

Thanks for saving Iris.

From Rob.

'You can't send that,' I said.

Rob pressed send/receive and grinned. 'I just did.'

CHAPTER 31

From: Jeneba Kah
Sent: 12th October 21.30 GMT

Subject: Iris

Hello Callum

Tell Rob I haven't been fighting with any crocodiles, but I'll remember to stick one in the eye if I ever do.

I am in hospital because I was hit by a truck. It skidded in the mud in the rainy season and broke my legs. I am in plaster waiting for them to mend.

I miss my village, but it is not so bad here in the hospital. I make friends with the new children that come into the ward. I pretend I am a doctor and try to guess what is wrong with them. In the evening Max sits on my bed and shows me pictures from his medical text books. He knows I want to be a doctor one day. He says he hopes I won't be as scary as Mama Binta though.

Mariama brought me some school work and chicken

Sky Hawk

Yassa today, so I am two times lucky. Chicken Yassa is her special recipe, my favourite. Mariama helped to look after me when I was little after my mother died, but she is also our school teacher too. I did an hour of maths with her. It was so much fun. Missing school is the worst thing about being in hospital.

Max has taken some pictures of my village to send to you. I hope you like the one of the fish my little brother caught for Iris.

What is Scotland like? Max said it is cold and wet and people only eat something called haggis. What is haggis anyway?

I will send you news of Iris every day.

Your friend

Jeneba

I showed Rob and Euan the email and photos next day at school.

'She's crazy,' said Rob. 'I'd go and break my legs just to have time *off* school.'

'Now that's what I call a fish,' said Euan. 'Imagine hauling that in.'

The photo showed a young boy no older than seven or eight holding up a long silver fish. The boy had to stand on tiptoes to keep the tail off the floor.

I flicked over the other pictures. Max had taken photos

of Jeneba's village. There were lots of small round huts and red brick buildings set around an open enclosure. The sky looked deep, deep blue, and the earth looked rust-red, dry and dusty. Under a fat-bellied tree sat a group of men hidden by the shade. In the open sunlight, women in brightly patterned clothes laid out fruits and vegetables to sell.

The last one was of Iris in Max's shed.

'It explains why we can't get a signal from Iris,' said Euan, 'if she's in a dark shed.'

'You can actually see the transmitter on her back and the long aerial poking out,' said Rob. 'She'd be dead by now if it wasn't for that.'

I nodded. 'She'll get better now,' I said, 'I just know she will.'

'We could send Jeneba some photos of Scotland,' said Euan.

'That's a great idea. We can take a photo of Iris's nest,' I said. 'I'll ask Mum to lend us her camera after school.'

Mum was in the kitchen doing the farm accounts at the table. She handed us the small digital camera she kept in her handbag. 'Make sure you take some of yourselves,' she said. 'Jeneba will want to know what you look like.'

Graham leaned across the table and helped himself to another huge piece of chocolate cake. 'She doesn't want to see Callum's ugly mug,' he said, dropping sticky crumbs over the accounts. 'It might crash the computer again. I'm surprised they have computers out in Uganda anyway.'

'The Gambia,' I said. 'Everywhere's got computers now.'

Mum flicked the crumbs from the papers. 'You're not doing much at the moment are you, Graham? Make yourself useful and take Callum and his friends out in the Land Rover to take photos of the farm before it gets dark.'

Graham rolled his eyes. 'Come on then,' he said. He picked up the Land Rover keys and headed out of the door.

Graham took us all over the farm. We were suddenly rally drivers. I'm sure Mum would've had a fit if she'd seen some of his handbrake turns.

But we did get some great photos of the farm. Graham took a picture of us with the mountains in the background and I photographed Iris's eyrie on the island in the loch. When we got back to the farmhouse, Mum had defrosted a haggis from the freezer for us and we photographed that too.

Later that evening, I downloaded the photos onto the computer and attached them to an email. I pressed the send button and our photos of Scotland went flying through cyberspace in a fraction of a second, all the way to Jeneba and Iris. All the way to Africa.

* * *

Each day after that, Jeneba wrote about Iris and sent more photos that Max had taken. Iris looked stronger as the days went by. Her feathers became shiny and glossy. There was a picture of her standing on a piece of wood, preening. It had to be a good sign. The old wound on her foot looked better too. The first pictures showed a thick lump of red flesh caked in dirt and the skin of her foot had been mottled and dark. But now, nearly two weeks later, the pictures showed the wound had almost healed.

Max had also taken more photos and short video clips of the village and the river. It made me feel as if I was really there. I could almost imagine myself walking down to the wide green river, where the long wooden fishing boats lay on the low tide mud. I could almost feel the hot African sun on my face and hear the sounds of the village, of children playing and women pounding sorghum and millet. I was almost there.

Almost.

That night there was one more email waiting for me.

Sky Hawk

From: Jeneba Kah
Sent: 25th October 20.40 GMT

Subject: Iris

Hello Callum,
Tomorrow is a very good day. Max has decided to set Iris free. He says she is strong now and needs to go back to the wild. He is going to release her at sunrise so she has the whole day to catch fish.

Doctor Jawara said he is taking the casts off my legs tomorrow, so I will be free too.

I am too excited to sleep. But Mama Binta said if I go to sleep she will let me see Max release Iris tomorrow. I think maybe Mama Binta isn't as fierce as she pretends to be.

I will write with good news tomorrow night.

Your friend, Jeneba.

CHAPTER 32

I rushed back home from school the next day to check on my emails. But there was nothing. I sat at my computer nearly all evening, but still no news from Jeneba. Not the next day, or the day after that. I sent emails to her but there was no reply.

I sat with Rob and Euan in the ICT suite at school. We were meant to be researching the French revolution.

'Maybe they've got electricity blackout,' said Euan.

'Have you checked on Iris?' said Rob. 'If they set her free we'd get a signal wouldn't we?'

I hadn't. It hadn't occurred to me.

Euan kept a look out for our teacher and I tapped in Iris's code.

Her signal came in strong and clear. It showed she'd flown

Sky Hawk

across the river from Jeneba's village on Monday morning, and spent the day along a small creek. The next day she'd flown north up the coast near the border of Senegal.

'They did it,' said Euan. 'They set her free then.'

'But we haven't heard from Jeneba,' I said.

Euan peered over my shoulder. 'We can only wait.'

We had to wait another week before we got an email.

From: Jeneba Kah
Sent: 3rd November 16.00 GMT

Subject: Iris

Hello Callum,
I am sorry I have not written, but I have not been well. I had the casts removed from my legs but the breaks in one leg are too bad, and my bones have not healed. I have a bad infection in it and this has been giving me a fever. Dr Jawara thinks he will have to amputate my leg.

My father visited the marabout last night. The marabout had another vision. This time, he saw me walking high above the world across an ocean of white cloud. My father thinks this means I am going to die. The marabout is never wrong. What scares me most is knowing I will never walk again.

I have sent a photo of Iris the day we set her free. Max let me do it. I was so happy to see her fly away on her

171

big strong wings. I wanted to follow her up into the sky. All the villagers were there and they cheered and clapped. Even Mama Binta's eyes were red and watery. She said she had some dust in her eye, but Max and I didn't believe her.

I will write when I can. I think of you and Iris every day.

Your friend, Jeneba.

I opened the attachment. It was a good photo, an action shot of Iris bursting from Jeneba's hands, huge wings outspread, and intense yellow eyes fixed on the sky above. It was almost an exact copy of the same moment when Iona and I had released Iris all those months ago. I should have felt the same thrill seeing the photo of Iris being released, but I didn't.

Instead, all I felt was a dull ache deep in my chest. Jeneba was thousands of miles away. She was very sick. And suddenly I felt completely and utterly helpless.

CHAPTER 33

'I don't see why they can't mend her legs,' said Rob. 'I mean, those racing drivers get badly smashed up and they have tons of metal in their legs. You see their X-rays in the papers, lots of screws and metal bars holding their bones together.'

'Maybe her family can't afford it,' said Euan.

'I've got four hundred pounds in savings,' I said. 'Mum said I wasn't to use it till I was older, but I'd use it for this.'

'I've got about twenty pounds,' said Rob. 'How much d'you think it would cost?'

'Write and ask,' said Euan. 'It's the only way we'll find out.'

We did write. Rob and Euan were playing computer games in my bedroom when we got our answer.

From: Max Walker
Sent: 6th November 14.20 GMT

Subject: Jeneba

Hello Callum,
This is Max writing to you. Jeneba is very sick right now. The fever has taken hold and Dr Jawara thinks she may have malaria as well. I am sorry but I can't show her your emails, it may give her false hope. In your country or America, maybe she could have surgery to mend her leg. But this is Africa. In this hospital I have worked with some of the best doctors and nurses I have ever met. They work hard against all the odds. But they can only work with what is given to them. This is a poor country and the hospitals cannot afford the equipment or the training for such complicated procedures.

But you and your friends are very kind to offer your own money.

Jeneba is a very special person. If there was anything we could do, we would.

Please keep writing to her, I know she likes your news.

Max.

'So that's it,' I said to Rob and Euan. 'There's nothing we can do. Iris gets to fly back to Scotland, but Jeneba will never walk again.'

Euan shrugged his shoulders and slumped back on my bed.

But Rob started laughing.

'What's so funny?' I said.

Sky Hawk

'Shut up, Rob,' said Euan giving him a kick.

Rob sat up on the bed, trying to catch his breath. 'It's simple isn't it?' he said. 'Jeneba can fly to Scotland, just like Iris.'

'Shut up, Rob.' I was angry with him now. 'That's not even funny. You're just sick.'

Rob laughed again and tapped my head. 'IN A PLANE . . . DUH-BRAIN!!'

'What?' I said.

'In a plane,' said Rob. 'We pay for her flight here, and then she can have treatment here in Scotland.'

'Brilliant,' I said.

'We'll need more money,' said Euan.

'Then we'll raise some money,' I said. 'Like the school fair. I'm sure Mum would bake some cakes.'

'And I could catch some fish,' said Euan.

'How much money would we need?' asked Rob.

I shrugged my shoulders. I had no idea.

'Get some paper and pens, Callum,' said Euan. 'Let's figure out how many stalls we need.'

CHAPTER 34

After a week of running around we were ready. Mum and Dad paid for the use of the village hall. Graham and I had driven around the farms and villages with the trailer and collected stuff people didn't want any more. We had several old TVs, a set of dinner plates, clothes, toys, and a big chicken run with two chickens to sell. Most people were glad to get rid of some things before Christmas.

Rob had printed out posters and leaflets advertising the fair, and he had cycled round all the houses posting them through letter boxes. On the leaflets he'd put a picture of Jeneba in her plaster casts, and in typical Rob style he'd written, 'Help us save Jeneba's leg before it gets the chop.'

Euan had gone out really early and managed to catch two fat trout from the river. Mum had baked enough cakes

Sky Hawk

and biscuits to feed a whole army, and Dad put his favourite whisky in the raffle. Hamish added to the raffle prizes with a year's free entry to the nature reserve he worked at. It seemed right that on the front of the nature reserve leaflet there was a photo of one of the ospreys that nested there.

It was nearly two o'clock and already I could see a queue of people outside the village hall waiting to come in. Mum fussed about with the tea urn and Euan's mum and Rob's mum set out some tables and chairs.

We were just about to open when Rob pushed his way through the back door. He was wheeling his bike with him.

'Take that out,' snapped his mum. 'We don't want mud in here.'

I looked across at Rob. His bike wasn't muddy. It wasn't muddy at all. It was sparkling clean, like new.

'Put it in the sale,' said Rob quietly.

'You're kidding,' I said.

He shook his head.

'It's got to sell for four hundred, OK? No less,' he said.

'You sure?' I couldn't believe it.

'Just do it,' he said. He ran his hand along the handlebars then turned and fled out of the hall, just as the first customers came into the fair.

* * *

It was hectic at first. People rummaged through piles of clothes and books and DVDs. The teas and coffees did a good trade, and Mum's cakes went down well. I ran a stall of second-hand CDs and electronic stuff. I even had Rob's bike next to the stall. There was lots of interest in it, but no one offered to buy it. Mum came over to bring me a drink and a slice of chocolate cake.

'It's going well,' smiled Mum.

'How much d'you think we've raised?' I asked.

Mum shrugged her shoulders. 'I don't know, but I reckon the teas and coffees alone have taken over a hundred pounds.'

She served the customers while I munched my cake. I wasn't really taking much notice of the stall until I heard Mum's voice.

'Hello, Mr McNair, how are you?'

I looked up. Iona's grandfather stood at the stall. He seemed smaller than I remembered, more stooped. He fumbled in his coat pocket for his wallet and held it out in his brown, leathery hands. They were shaking badly.

'I'll take the bike,' he said.

Mum smiled. 'It's a wee bit expensive, I'm afraid,' she said.

Sky Hawk

Mr McNair opened his wallet and pulled out some notes. He laid them on the table counting up in twenties.

'Mr McNair . . . ' protested Mum.

'It's all there,' he said. 'Four hundred pounds.'

'It's a lot of money . . . you can't afford it,' said Mum.

Mr McNair pulled out another ten pound note and slapped it on the table. 'And I'll take the two trout on the next stall too.'

He put the fish in a plastic bag, took Rob's bike by the handlebars, walked out of the hall, and was gone.

Mum picked up the money and stared after him.

I didn't know how I was going to tell Rob.

CHAPTER 35

By five o'clock the village hall was empty. There were some boxes of books and a bag of old clothes left, but we had sold most of the stuff.

Mum made a fresh pot of tea and we sat down to finish the rest of the cakes and total up the money. There were piles of it, coins stacked up and bags of notes. Rob and his dad joined us right at the end.

'Well, the grand total is,' said Hamish with a big grin, 'one thousand, four hundred and sixty-two pounds and eight pence.'

All the adults cheered. But I didn't. It wasn't enough. We'd found out at the end of the week that it wasn't that simple to just fly Jeneba out here. She wasn't British so her treatment would have to be paid for, and it would cost tens of thousands of pounds. I went to sit on the same table with Rob and Euan.

'It's a start,' said Rob. 'We can raise more.'

I nodded. I didn't want Rob to think he'd sold his bike for nothing.

'It sold then?' said Rob.

'I'm sorry,' I said.

Euan was shaking his head in disbelief. 'I still can't believe you did it,' he said. 'I mean, that bike was part of you. What'll you do without wheels?'

Rob slumped further in his seat. 'I've still got legs,' he said with a half laugh. 'I guess I'll have to take up running instead.'

It was dark by the time we'd cleared the hall and put the chairs away. We walked out into the car park while Mum locked up the village hall.

Euan nudged me. 'Over there,' he said.

I looked across the road. Under the street lamp stood Mr McNair with Rob's bike.

Rob noticed too, but kept his head down and followed his dad to the car.

Mr McNair wheeled the bike over to us and stared at Rob from under his bushy eyebrows. There was an awkward silence.

CHAPTER 35

Mr McNair didn't take his eyes off Rob. 'So you're Rob, the boy with the mean mouth and the big wheels,' he said. 'Mean mouth and no manners, that's what I once heard.'

Mr McNair was so close to us. I could see the spidery veins across the white of his eyes and the lined bristly skin of his face.

Rob glanced at his bike and then at the ground.

'Come on,' said Rob's dad, pulling Rob away.

Mr McNair pushed the bike closer, almost touching Rob. The tick . . . tick . . . tick of the turning wheels sounded loud in the silence. 'It seems,' he said, 'you've got your manners back.'

Rob turned to look at him.

Mr McNair glared at him gruffly. 'You'd better have your bike back too. It's no use to me.' He pushed the bike into Rob's hands and patted the plastic bag with Euan's fish. 'I'll keep these though. It's a long time since I had a bit of fresh trout.' He tucked the bag under his arm and shuffled away up the dark street.

'Wait,' called Mum. 'Mr McNair . . . maybe I could cook those trout for you. With a bit of parsley and butter . . . '

Mr McNair turned and nodded. 'Aye, Mrs McGregor, that'd be grand.'

I glanced at Rob. He was speechless.

Sky Hawk

'You'll have to ride home now,' said his dad.

Rob grinned, big and wide. He swung his leg over the bike and circled round the car park, shooting up and down the grassy banks.

'WATCH OUT!' I yelled.

A car shot into the car park and screeched to a stop beside us, headlights full on, blaring. A young woman, blonde and smartly dressed, opened the door.

'Is this the village hall?' she asked.

Dad nodded.

She smiled at all of us. 'I'm looking for Callum McGregor,' she said.

Everyone looked in my direction. 'That's me,' I said.

She held out her hand. 'Karen Burrows,' she said. 'I heard there's a village fair here.'

'I'm afraid it's finished,' I said. 'You've missed it.'

'Oh?' She raised her eyebrows. 'No matter. I'm from the *Highland Chronicle*. I want to write a piece on your fundraising.'

I knew the *Highland Chronicle*, it was the local paper for the area, with local news and events and adverts. 'I'm sorry, but you're a bit late,' I said.

'It's not that,' she said. She reached into the car for her notepad and voice recorder. She smiled at me, a sort of smile that held known secrets. 'It's just that I heard you're raising money for an African girl . . . '

I nodded, but a deep knot tightened in the pit of my stomach.

' . . . and,' she said, 'it's all because of an osprey you saved, here, in Scotland. Is that true?'

Chapter 36

'How did that reporter know all about the osprey?' I said. 'We told no one.'

We stood in the village hall car park watching the taillights of Karen Burrows's car disappear up the road.

Euan glanced at his dad, then at me. 'I think it was me,' he said. 'I didn't mean to. I was talking about the fundraising to one of the people who deliver the papers to Dad's shop. I said the Gambian girl had found an osprey, but I never said it was from here. I hardly mentioned it.'

'Well, that woman's going to put it in the papers next week,' I said.

Hamish stepped between us. 'She doesn't know where you live,' he said.

'Not yet,' I said angrily. 'I bet we'll soon have people

snooping all over the farm. Once Iris comes back, she'll never be safe again.'

'It's only a local rag running the story,' said Dad. 'It's not like it's going to be national news.'

'Well, it only takes one person to steal the eggs,' I snapped.

Dad opened the car door. 'Come on, let's go home. It's been a long day.'

The *Chronicle* ran the story on Monday. Dad showed me the paper when I got home from school. I was relieved to see it wasn't on the front page. It was a small article near the middle of the paper showing a picture of an osprey and the poster Rob had made.

'See?' said Dad. 'Blink and you'd miss it.'

'I suppose you're right,' I said.

'I'm always right,' Dad said with a grin.

I tapped in Iris's code on the computer. I wanted to tell her it was safe to come back. I wanted her to come back here, to the farm. I checked on her every day now. It was as if keeping that connection kept her alive, as if she knew I was there, watching her. She was still in The Gambia, near the coast. The photos showed long wide sandy beaches

and river deltas with mangrove forest. Her signal had criss-
crossed the same river inlet for nearly a week. Hamish said
the first week after release was the hardest. It was make
or break. But Iris had made it. She was still flying, still
hunting. She was alive.

I missed her. I hadn't been to look at the eyrie for ages.
I promised myself I would get up early the next day and go
and check it for storm damage. It was an excuse to go up
there, really. After a week of organizing the fundraising fair,
I just wanted some time alone, up on the hills. I put out my
fleece jacket and thick socks and set the alarm for six thirty.

I woke before the alarm. It was still dark outside and silent.
Fern patterns of frost sparkled on the window in the light
of a half moon. I got up, dressed in several layers of clothes
and went down to the kitchen. It was warm from the heat
of the cooking range. I tore off a piece of bread from the
loaf Mum had left out, put on my boots, and slipped out
into the yard.

The lights were on in one of the barns. Dad was up
already, checking on the sheep. I heard the rustle of straw as
Kip came out to greet me. His tail thumped on the wooden
sides of the kennel, his breath misted white in the cold air.

'Come on then,' I said. I leaned down to unclip his chain and ruffled my hands through his thick winter coat. He licked my face and barked. I put my hand over his muzzle. 'Shh, Kip, no noise.' And as if he understood, he padded silently ahead of me, out of the yard and up the track leading to the loch.

I loved the farm before the dawn. It was a different place. Frost-crusted puddles reflected the moonlight and lit up the path. The outline of hills was soft and dark, like waves on a midnight sea, and the woods were a smudge of blackness so deep it looked impossible to enter. There were no colours, only the deepness of blue.

I was out of breath by the time I reached the loch. The moon was a shining white ball in the water. I couldn't make out the eyrie very well. It was almost hidden from the ground. If you didn't know it was there, you'd miss it.

I thought of going to the tree-house, just to look. But I couldn't do it. Iona and I never did get to sleep the night up there. I sat down on a flat rock jutting out over the loch, and chewed on the piece of bread from my pocket.

A pale light was spreading across the eastern sky and the night farm was fading. Colours slowly merged into the day, the pale greens of the fields, peaty browns of the loch, and strips of promised sunlight beneath the clouds.

Sky Hawk

Maybe Iona and I would have sat here, on this rock, and watched a dawn just like this. Maybe.

I threw Kip the crust. 'Come on,' I said. 'I've got school and you've got work to do with Dad today.'

I jumped down from the rock and whistled to Kip, but he was standing absolutely still, staring into the valley below, his ears pricked.

'Come on, Kip,' I said. He followed me down the path by the river, but stopped again. A low growl built in his throat and his hackles were raised.

Kip saw the man before I did.

We hardly ever had walkers and ramblers on our farm. Not at this time in the morning, anyway.

We met on a corner, where the bend was steep. Small loose stones skittered under the man's feet.

'Hello,' he said. He had a posh, southern accent. He smiled as if he was expecting to meet me here. 'Callum McGregor, is it?'

I nodded.

He held up his camera. It was one of those big ones with a huge lens. 'D'you mind if I take your photo? I'm doing a feature on the osprey you saved.'

I could feel Kip press against my leg. 'I've got to go,' I said. 'I've lost some sheep.' I pushed past him and ran down the track. When I turned around at the bottom of the hill, I could see him coming down the track too. I ran on, as fast as I could, back home. I had to tell Mum and Dad and Hamish. I had to tell them there was someone snooping on the farm.

I burst into the yard. Mum was grim faced by the back door.

'Euan's dad has just been on the phone,' she said. 'There are TV cameras and journalists swarming all over the village. It's you they want to talk to. We'd better get down there.'

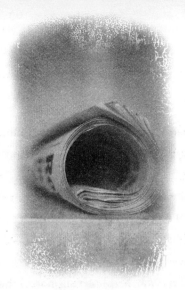

CHAPTER 37

D ad pulled up in the road behind the village hall. We could see the car park was full of camera crews and journalists. Mrs Wicklow was standing in the back entrance of the village hall beckoning us in. Mum, Dad, Graham, and I scrambled over the back fence into the village hall.

It looked as if everyone from the village was crammed in there. I could hear reporters knocking at the door.

'It's big news,' said Euan's dad. 'Seems everyone wants to know.' He shook his head. 'There are more reporters on the way here. There's even a television crew from CNN. It's world news now.'

'I'm sorry,' said Euan.

Mrs Wicklow put her hand on my arm. 'We won't tell them about the osprey on your farm.'

I looked round the faces staring at me. 'Oh, so everyone knows, do they? I may as well take the reporters up to the loch now.'

'But they don't know where the nest is,' said Euan.

'And none of us are going to show them,' said Rob's dad.

I glared at them all. 'It won't take them long to work it out. Iris will never be safe again.'

Just then there was a splintering sound and the doors were flung open. Reporters and cameramen surged into the hall.

Euan caught me by the arm. 'Don't say a word,' he whispered. 'Rob and I have got a plan. Wait for us. Don't say a word.' I watched them push their way through the crowd and go out into the open air.

'There he is.'

I turned to see the tall reporter I'd met on the hill striding towards me. He held out a hand. 'Here's the boy who can tell us all about it.'

I backed away. Suddenly all the cameras were pointing at me. About ten people were asking questions all at once. Everything seemed to slow down and speed up at the same time. I could hear Mum calling me from the back of the crowd. She sounded far away. A woman took me gently by the arm and led me outside.

Sky Hawk

'This way, Callum,' she smiled. I followed her, squeezing through jackets, coats, and cameras.

I found myself standing in front of a TV camera, next to the smiling lady. 'We're going on live TV,' she said. 'Everyone wants to know your remarkable story.'

The cameras were running and she was talking. And I was telling her about Jeneba, about the fundraising to pay for her operation over here and about the Gambian villagers finding the osprey from the satellite signals in the mangrove forests.

'And this osprey,' she said, still smiling. 'How did you get to know about this osprey?'

My mouth went dry. I stalled. There were microphones all pointing at me. Out of the corner of my eye I saw a truck screech into the car park. I saw Rob and Euan and Hamish running towards me. It all seemed to be happening in slow motion.

'This osprey,' said the smiling lady. 'Did you find it here, in this valley?'

I opened my mouth to speak as Hamish wrapped his arm around me and stepped in front of the camera.

'No,' Hamish said. 'Callum and his friends here have been following one of the ospreys at the nature reserve where I work. We had a breeding pair there last summer.

As you know they're endangered birds. We have CCTV and razor wire to protect them. And if you'd all like to come with me to the reserve, I can show you the nest right now.'

I sank into a chair. I felt exhausted. The last of the reporters' cars had left the yard, following Hamish on the fifteen mile trip to the nature reserve.

Mum made cups of tea for everyone from the village and soon it became a bit of an early morning party.

Rob's dad gave me a pat on the back. 'The osprey on your farm is our secret too. We all stick together for something like this.'

'How did everyone know?' I said.

'No one did until today,' said Rob's dad. 'But Mr McNair saw the journalists arrive early this morning. He saw a reporter heading up to the loch and guessed the osprey nest was up there. McNair told Mrs Beatty at the post office and she told everyone else. That's why we all came here, to stop the reporters snooping about your farm. We told them you were with us.'

'It was a close one,' said Rob.

Euan was pale. 'We almost didn't make it.'

Sky Hawk

'How did he know?' I said. 'How did Mr McNair know about the ospreys on our farm?'

Mum put a cup of tea on the table beside me and sat down. 'He found a box of Iona's things, her drawings and pictures. He remembered his father telling him there were once ospreys in the valley too. I guess he put two and two together.'

Rob's mum arrived at the hall with some bacon and eggs. 'I may as well make you all breakfast,' she said. 'You're late for school already. I don't think another half hour will hurt.'

We were finishing our bacon and eggs when a car arrived at the village hall. The tall reporter I had met before came through the door.

Mum started clearing the ketchup and brown sauce bottles away. 'They've all got school now, I'm afraid,' she said.

The man took out his mobile and scrolled through his messages. 'I just need to check a few things with Callum. That's all.'

'Well, he's not got long, so be quick.' Mum pulled on her coat and picked up her handbag.

The man smiled at her. 'I just need to check the charity number for Jeneba. Our news-desk has already received donations of money towards her treatment in the UK.'

Mum sat down, clutching her handbag. 'How much money are we talking here?'

The reporter scrolled through his messages again. 'Well, it's only an hour since the newscast went out, but there are donations already in the region of about ten thousand pounds.'

I almost choked on my bacon. 'Ten thousand?'

'Yup,' said the man. He scrolled down the messages again. 'Oh, and there's an orthopaedic surgeon in London, mad keen on birds. He's offered to do the operation free.'

CHAPTER 38

More money came in over the rest of the day, and the following days after that. People from all over the world gave money, from Canada, Japan, France, and America. One of the newspapers paid for someone to be in charge of the charity for Jeneba and arrange her trip over here.

It all happened so quickly. It was out of our hands, out of our control. There were photos of Jeneba in the Gambian hospital bed, photos of the village and the river. My words and the story had been changed for magazine and newspaper articles. Jeneba was suddenly everyone else's friend, everyone else's property. I was happy for her. But I felt I'd lost her. She hadn't answered any emails. I had to find out what was happening from the newspapers.

'Be patient,' said Mum. 'She probably feels the same way too. Suddenly everyone's taking charge of her life. She's been sick remember.'

I waited, and I needn't have worried. Jeneba sent an email:

From: Jeneba Kah
Sent: 1st December 13.30

Subject: Flying like Iris

Hello Callum,
I am sorry I have not written. It has taken much time to clear the infection in my leg. But I am well to travel now. When Dr Jawara told me I was going to Britain to mend my leg I could not believe it. I cannot thank your village enough for helping me. I keep thinking, maybe the marabout is wrong this time. Maybe his dream of me walking across the ocean of clouds will not come true. Maybe I will really walk again.

There have been lots of journalists here too. Mama Binta says they are worse than the village goats just wandering into the hospital when they like. But I like them. They are funny. They bring books and pens and toys for us.

Everything has happened so fast. Tomorrow I fly to London. I am so excited. No one from the village has been in an aeroplane before. I need a nurse to travel with me, so Mama Binta is coming too. Dr Jawara said he feels sorry for all the British doctors! I think Mama Binta heard, because Dr Jawara has been hiding from her all day.

Sky Hawk

It is also a sad day tomorrow because Max is going back to America. We are having a party for him today. Max gave me his medical books. He said I'm going to need them when I am a doctor. And I will be a doctor one day, Callum, I will. The money you raised is enough to send me to school and then college. I've never seen Mama Binta smile as big as she did when she found out. Mama Binta says she always wanted to be a doctor. I think she would have been the best doctor too.

Maybe I can come and see you in Scotland. Is it far from London? I would love to see the mountains and the rivers in your photos. I hope I will see Iris again one day too.

Your friend

Jeneba.

CHAPTER 39

The next few months went by so fast. At Christmas, people from the village sent Mama Binta and Jeneba clothes and books. Mama Binta phoned us to say Jeneba was doing well, but had had four operations on her leg already and was very tired most of the time. I'd sent a Christmas card and a letter, but it wasn't until New Year that I got a letter back from her.

4th January

Happy New Year, Callum.

I am writing from my hospital bed. I don't have a computer so I can't email you, but maybe when I am strong enough Mama Binta

can take me to the internet café on the
street below my window.

Please thank the people from your village
for the kind gifts. Mama Binta was very
happy with the jumpers you sent. She finds
England so cold. She is wearing all three of
the jumpers all at the same time!!!

We had a great surprise at New Year.
Max came to see us. He is staying with
friends in London. He says Scotland is the
best place in the world for New Year. He
tried to teach us a song called 'Auld Lang
Syne', but he only knew the first line. It
didn't stop him getting all the doctors and
nurses singing and dancing along. Even Mama
Binta joined in, and I didn't know she could
dance.

The streets here are very pretty with
bright lights. There is even a flashing
reindeer on the shop opposite my room. Mama
Binta says she doesn't know if it is day or
night in London. She misses the dark skies of
home.

Today I saw snow. One of the nurses took me
outside in the street. I watched it fall

from the sky and tried to catch it in my
mouth. I was covered all over in big white
snowflakes. They landed in my hair and on my
face and on my clothes. Close up, they look
like little stars, millions and millions
of them. The nurse told me that not one
snowflake is ever the same. She said they
are all different, all special.

Is there snow in Scotland?

I hope one day soon I can come and see you.

Your friend
Jeneba.

It didn't snow properly in Scotland until late February.
When it did, it was thick and deep. The farm and hills and
village were white with it. School was cancelled for nearly
a week, and Rob and Euan and I spent most of the time
tobogganing on the hills behind the village.

We checked on Iris's position in The Gambia every day.
She was still on the same river creek she'd been on for
weeks. Then, in the middle of March when most of the
snow had thawed from the hills, leaving only dirty grey
patches in the deepest gullies, Iris's signal changed. She left

Sky Hawk

The Gambia and was flying north, up along the coastline of Senegal.

After all those months in Africa, she was on her way, back here.

To Scotland.

Every chance we got, we followed her journey. We were in the school ICT rooms at most break-times and lunch until Mrs Wicklow found us out. We couldn't believe it when she asked us if she could put Iris's journey up on the whiteboard, so the whole class could follow her too. She'd stop lessons half an hour early so we could look at photos of dawn in the desert, of Berber shepherds in the high Atlas Mountains, flocks of birds on estuary mud flats, and cattle grazing green lowland pastures.

Hamish was following Iris's journey too. I met him after school one day to check on the eyrie up at the loch. The sky was overcast and still. Thin wisps of mist clung to the tops of the pine trees, and the oak and wild cherry were bare-leaved, waiting for spring.

'Iris has left Spain,' I said. 'She's flying in a straight line, north, across the Bay of Biscay.'

Hamish nodded. 'I'm surprised she's flying over open water. Ospreys usually come up through France and rest on the way. I guess she's in a hurry to get back to the nest.'

'Will she be OK?' I said.

'Other birds have done that route before.' He stopped at the loch-side and pulled out his binoculars. 'She could be here within the week,' he said.

'What day d'you reckon she'll get here?' I asked.

But Hamish wasn't listening. His binoculars were fixed on the cluster of pines on the rocky island, and he had a big grin on his face.

'What is it?' I said.

'Here,' he said, passing me the binoculars and pointing across the loch. 'Take a look at that.'

CHAPTER 40

I couldn't wait to tell Jeneba what Hamish and I had
seen on the loch, and the next day I had my chance. I
received an email from Jeneba:

From: Jeneba
Sent: 31st March 20.30 GMT

Subject: Good News

Hello Callum,
The doctors say I am strong enough to go out and about
now, so Mama Binta has pushed me in my wheelchair to
the internet café so I can write to you.

Mama Binta and I are coming to Scotland, TOMORROW!
I am so excited. It is so sudden, but one of the doctors
said he can drive us up to you because he is visiting his
family in Scotland for the weekend.

I will not get any sleep tonight. I can't stop thinking of meeting you.

Your friend

Jeneba.

'Mum!' I yelled. 'Dad!' I ran downstairs and jumped the last five steps. 'Mum!' I burst into the kitchen where Mum and Dad were watching TV. 'They're coming tomorrow night. I've just got an email.'

Mum jumped up. 'Tomorrow, are you sure?'

I nodded.

'Heavens!' She picked up the telephone. 'I'd better let everyone know. We've got a party to get ready.'

I ran back upstairs so I could email Jeneba. I was bursting to tell her *my* news:

From: Callum
Sent: 31st March 20.44 GMT

Subject: Racing Iris

Hello Jeneba,
That's brilliant. I can't believe you are coming to Scotland tomorrow. Word is spreading around the village, and we're having a big party for you and Mama Binta when you get here.

I have two bits of good news for you too.

Sky Hawk

Iris's mate is back! Hamish and I saw him yesterday up at the loch collecting sticks for the nest. I wonder where he spent the winter. Maybe he was in your country too. But now he's back here, on the farm and waiting for Iris.

And the other great news is about Iris. She's almost here. She made it to the south-west tip of Ireland this evening. She flew all the way across the sea from Spain. Hamish thinks she got blown off course, because ospreys usually come up through France and the south of England. She must be exhausted. She flew non-stop for over seven hundred miles and it took her less than two days!

I've worked out that if she sets out really early tomorrow and flies non-stop like she did before, she could be on our farm by ten tomorrow night.

You'd better hurry. She might even beat you here!

I can't wait until tomorrow.

Callum.

P.S. I hope Mama Binta's practised for the Scottish Dancing.

CHAPTER 41

The next morning I rolled out of bed and checked on Iris's position. I grinned. She was on her way.

She'd made an early start and was flying up the east coast of Ireland. I ran down the stairs into the kitchen to tell Mum and Dad, but was met by Graham in the hall.

'I wouldn't go in there if I were you,' said Graham. 'Mum's in panic mode. She's sending me to the shops to get a ton of flour for making cakes.'

I peered in through the door.

'There you are, Callum,' snapped Mum. She was madly scrubbing the kitchen floor. 'I hope your room's tidy, you'll need to strip the beds, and clean the bathroom, we'll need extra blankets from the attic and . . . oh, Graham, haven't you gone yet?'

Sky Hawk

'Cool down, Mum,' called Graham. 'Last minute parties are always the best, trust me.'

'But there's all the food to think about . . . and the music,' said Mum.

Dad walked in from the yard.

'It's all sorted. Everyone from the village is bringing some food and drink. The bar will be open. There'll be more than enough.'

'And Flint's girlfriend is bringing her band,' said Graham. 'There'll be Scottish dancing and everything. Even Euan's dad is playing his bagpipes to welcome them in.'

'But . . . ' said Mum.

'Trust us,' smiled Dad. 'It'll be fine.'

We were busy all day. Rob, Euan, and I helped Dad get the village hall ready for the party. We put out tables and chairs, hung bunting from the roof and decorated the stage. More people came in the afternoon to help and deliver food. Euan's dad practised his bagpipes and soon there was quite a party happening. Rob got a football match started between the kids and the parents, and even Mrs Wicklow joined in.

When everything was finished and done, Dad and I went

back home to get changed for the party.

'You've not got long,' said Mum as we walked through the door. 'I've just had a phone call. Jeneba and Mama Binta have made good time. They'll be here within the hour.'

I rushed upstairs. I felt suddenly so nervous. I hadn't met Jeneba face to face before. What if she didn't like me? What if after all the excitement our village was a huge let-down for her?

I changed and went down into the kitchen where Dad was watching the six o'clock news. He was in his jeans and blue checked shirt, and was brushing his hair in front of the telly.

'Come on,' said Mum. 'Hamish is giving us a lift. I can see him coming up the lane now.'

'I'll just catch the weather,' said Dad.

I sat down beside him jiggling my feet under the table. I couldn't keep still.

The weather man stood in front of a big map of Britain sweeping his hand across Scotland.

'*Northern Scotland will enjoy a spell of settled weather over the next couple of days,*' he said. '*But I can't say the same for the south and west of England. There's a severe weather warning in place for the Bristol Channel and the Irish Sea. Just look at those isobars packed together. We can expect gale-force winds with those.*'

Sky Hawk

I stared at the map. It was real time. A storm was moving across the Irish Sea now. Iris was out there, in those winds, in that storm.

I raced up to my room and switched on the computer. Maybe she had made it ahead of the storm. Maybe she was already sheltering on land somewhere.

My heart hammered in my chest.

The computer flickered into life.

'Come on,' I said. 'Come on.'

But there was no signal.

None.

It was as if she'd vanished off the face of the earth.

I tried to block out thoughts of the storm, but all I could see and hear were screaming winds and high, mountainous seas.

Iris sensed the storm long before the dark clouds massed and formed above her. She tilted away from the curling threads of wind, flying hard and fast. But the storm was faster still. It ploughed across the sea, churning it into green-grey troughs and peaks of foam-tipped waves.

The storm-winds pounded Iris. Salt spray clogged her tattered flight feathers. The air and sea were white with foam. It stuck to her face and reached deep into the soft downy layers. She felt heavy, waterlogged. She was flying to stay alive.

The waves peaked and crested beneath her in a blur of white-streaked surf. One wave rose beside her, higher than the rest. Higher and higher, its peak curled and tumbled, folding over Iris, sealing her in a tube of thundering whiteness. Her wingtips brushed the wall of surf. It broke onto her, pushing her into the sea. Over and over she turned. Salt water rushed into her beak and nostrils.

She bobbed up to the surface and shook the water from her head. The straps the humans had tied to her floated loose around her. She clawed at them, pushing them down, down into the water. Iris launched upwards as another wave curled high above her. Her feet still trailed beneath the surface as it came crashing down towards her in a surging mass of surf and foam and spray.

CHAPTER 42

'We've lost her,' I said to Hamish as he came into the kitchen. 'There's no signal.'

'I know,' he said quietly. 'I've just checked too.' He frowned, the lines on his forehead running into a deep crease. 'These transmitters are designed to fall off eventually. Sometimes they just go wrong, they stop working.'

'It was working this morning,' I said. 'She's gone, Hamish, gone.'

Hamish gave out a long sigh.

'All I'm saying is,' he said, 'we can't give up hope. Not yet.'

I slumped back into my seat and shook my head. 'She hasn't made it.'

Dad put his arms round my shoulders. 'Come on,' he

said. 'I know this is a shock, but we have to get you to the party to welcome Jeneba.'

I nodded and followed them out to Hamish's Land Rover. The hills and fields passed in a blur beside me and soon Hamish was pulling into the crowded car park of the village hall.

Mum turned round and squeezed my hand. 'Deep breath,' she smiled. 'Do this for Jeneba, OK?'

I stepped out of the car.

'There you are, Callum,' shouted Rob.

I turned to see Rob and Euan pushing their way towards me.

'Where've you been?' said Euan. 'You almost didn't make it.'

Rob's dad's voice shouted over everyone. He was standing on the top of his pick-up truck. 'They're here,' he yelled. 'I can see them, coming up the road.'

Suddenly everyone was gathering together, children and adults all laughing and shouting. No one was in charge, but we all somehow formed two long lines up the road to welcome Jeneba and Mama Binta in.

Their car swept them into the village and up to the hall. Mama Binta stepped out onto the pavement, wrapped in shawls and blankets. Everyone was cheering and clapping, and I guessed for probably the first time in her life, Mama Binta was utterly speechless.

Jeneba was waving madly through the window. I just watched as Mum and Hamish helped her out and into her wheelchair. I couldn't believe she was really here, in Scotland, in our village. Suddenly I couldn't think of a thing to say. I backed away into the crowd.

'Callum McGregor?' Mama Binta was marching towards me. 'Callum McGregor, what you doing hiding in there,' she bawled. 'You get your skinny backside out here.'

I was being pushed forward by the crowd towards Jeneba and Mama Binta. Jeneba was grinning and Mama Binta put her arms around me and gave me a bone-crushing hug. 'Well, Callum,' she said. 'I've been looking forward to this day for a *long, long* time.'

Everyone was cheering and clapping again.

I pushed the wheelchair, and Jeneba and I led the way into the hall.

CHAPTER 43

Graham was right. It was a great party. Flint's girlfriend got everyone to find partners and started calling the dances. Mama Binta was up there swinging round on Hamish's arm. Rob and Euan and some of the girls from school pushed Jeneba round and round in the wheelchair. Music played, people ate and drank and danced well into the night.

The only person who wasn't there was Mr McNair. Mum had offered to give him a lift, but he didn't come. He told Mum he'd given up dancing a long time ago.

'I'm really sorry about Iris,' said Jeneba. 'Hamish told me.'

We sat beside each other at the back of the hall while the band worked the dancers faster and faster.

Sky Hawk

'I wanted to see her so much,' I said.

Jeneba nodded. 'I kept looking into the sky today. I hoped to see her on the way here.'

I looked across at Jeneba. It struck me how real she was, not just a name at the end of an email. She was actually here, right now, after all that had happened.

'I'm glad you're here,' I said.

Jeneba smiled at me. She reached across and squeezed my hand, tight. 'I am too.'

Dad flopped down in a chair next to us. Sweat was pouring down his face. 'Mama Binta can't half dance,' he said. We looked across to see someone else twirl Mama Binta by the arm and whisk her away across the dance floor.

'You both look shattered,' said Dad. 'It's gone twelve. Come on, you two, let's get you home. I've got to check on the sheep anyway.'

Hamish drove us home. We huddled under coats in the chill night air. The mountains were blue-black against the midnight sky. A thin veil of mist circled the moon like a halo.

'Go on in and make yourselves a hot chocolate,' said Dad. 'I won't be long checking the sheep.'

Hamish helped Jeneba down from the Land Rover. Jeneba propped her crutches under her arms. 'Look,' she said.

'The doctors say I can try to walk a little on crutches now.'

'That's just amazing,' smiled Hamish. He helped her across the stony yard to the kitchen door.

'Hamish?' I said.

He turned to look at me.

'Will you take us up on the hill tomorrow morning, just us?' I said. 'I promised to show Jeneba the eyrie.'

Hamish nodded. 'I'm working tomorrow, so it'll have to be early.'

'We'll be ready,' I said.

I followed Jeneba slowly into the kitchen.

'D'you want hot chocolate?' I asked.

Jeneba nodded. 'I love hot chocolate. I have it all the time at the hospital.'

She sat down at the table while I boiled the milk and stirred in the chocolate powder. She looked tired, her head propped in her hands, her eyes half closed. I felt tired too. It had been a long day.

'Here,' I said. I pushed Mum's pile of laundry and Dad's paper to the side, and put the steaming hot chocolate in front of her.

I sat down and wrapped my hands around my own mug letting the warmth seep through me. I was so tired I felt I could have stayed like that, just staring into the steam. I watched it spiral slowly upwards. It made me think of Iris circling high in the sky.

The swirling drift of steam stretched its feathery wings and flew in slow lazy circles into the air. It rose higher and higher and brushed my face with the tips of its wings. It wheeled over the newspaper and ironed shirts on the kitchen table. It soared across the white buttoned mountains and worded valleys. It drifted towards me again. I wanted to hold it in my hands, hold it and keep it for ever. I reached out my fingers but it slipped through them, dissolving into wispy threads and was gone.

Jeneba was looking at me, smiling. 'You know,' she said, 'maybe you are like the marabout. Maybe the bird spirit, she flies to you too.'

CHAPTER 44

I woke early the next morning. I got up from my bed and peered out of the window. A fog had swallowed us up in the night. I couldn't see a thing outside, just bright whiteness. The farmhouse was strangely quiet and still. I slipped on my jumper and jeans and padded into the kitchen.

Mum was getting breakfast things ready and Dad was sitting in a chair holding his head in his hands.

'I can't party like I used to,' he groaned.

Mum winked at me and put a plate of sausages and hash browns in front of him. 'Get that down you,' she said.

Feet sounded on the yard outside and Graham clumped in through the door.

'Shh!' whispered Mum. 'Jeneba and Mama Binta are still asleep.'

Sky Hawk

Graham sat down next to Dad. 'You can't see the nose on your face in that fog.' He reached over and grabbed a sausage from Dad's plate. 'Can't let good food go to waste,' he said stuffing it in his mouth.

'Here they are,' said Mum.

I turned to see Mama Binta helping Jeneba through the door. Mum pulled out a chair with a soft cushion and helped Jeneba sit down.

Jeneba was dressed in what looked like about ten jumpers, a fleece, a pair of thick trousers, woolly walking socks and an old blue bobble hat.

'What do you think, Callum?' she said. 'Am I ready for the mountains?'

I laughed. 'I think you'll make base camp on Everest in those.'

Mama Binta pulled her shawl around her shoulders and leaned against the warm cooking range. 'You won't find me up any mountains,' she shivered. 'It's like living in a big freezer out there.'

'There's no point going to the loch until after lunch anyway,' said Dad. 'The fog might clear by then.'

'But Dad . . . ' I said. 'It doesn't give us much time. Rob's mum and dad are taking Jeneba out this afternoon to the woollen mills, and anyway . . . ' I was interrupted by a muffled engine arriving in the yard, and headlights circled by fog. ' . . . Hamish is here.'

Hamish knocked on the door and walked into the kitchen. 'Morning, all,' he grinned. He turned to Jeneba and me. 'Are you ready to go and take a look at the eyrie?' We both nodded. 'Come on then, lass,' said Hamish. He held out his hands to her. 'Let's get you into the Land Rover.'

'But they haven't had breakfast,' Mum said.

'We'll have it later,' I called, 'I've got to get something.' I rushed up to my room to look for my binoculars. I hadn't used them since last year. I grabbed them from the top of the wardrobe and went back down to the kitchen.

'You won't see much with those,' said Dad as I went out of the door.

The fog pressed against me, damp and heavy, as I crossed the yard.

Jeneba was already in the front seat. I opened the door and climbed in next to her, the crutches between us. The Land Rover rumbled into life and Hamish drove out of the yard and up the field track towards the loch. Sheep loomed out of the mist and stared at us as we passed. Hamish tried switching his headlights on full beam, but the glare bounced back at us. The track swung around the curve of the hill and started to climb steeply upwards.

Sky Hawk

'I think we've missed the track to the loch,' I said.

Hamish peered into the mist. 'Are you sure?'

I looked all around, but there was nothing but whiteness. No landmarks, nothing.

'I think so,' I said. 'We shouldn't be climbing so steeply.'

The Land Rover side-slipped in the muddy track. 'I can't turn round yet,' Hamish muttered. 'We'll go on. If I stop now, we might get stuck.'

He drove slowly on, bumping over the rock and stones. Jeneba put her hands out on the dashboard to steady herself. Below my window, the edge of the track tumbled away into swirling mist.

'At least I can say I've been on the mountains,' Jeneba said, 'even if I can't see them.'

'It's a bit brighter in front,' said Hamish.

The ground was flatter and covered by coarse grass. It was lighter and brighter all around. Colour had seeped into the world again. The outline of an orange sun pierced the mist above. Hamish edged the Land Rover on through the thinning whiteness and out into bright sunshine and blue, blue sky.

He turned the engine off and we sat in silence looking around.

Hamish whistled softly. 'You don't see something like this every day.'

The tops of the mountains pushed above the mist-filled valleys. They rose like islands above a sea of white cloud.

'Please help me down,' said Jeneba.

She was quiet, a slight frown on her face.

'I want to walk,' she said.

Hamish helped her down from the Land Rover. I passed her the crutches, but she shook her head. 'I must do this on my own.'

She spread her arms to steady herself. And, slowly, she took her first steps, one foot in front of the other.

'You're walking,' I shouted, 'you're really walking.'

She stopped and turned to me and smiled the biggest smile. 'Look, Callum,' she said. 'The marabout, he was right.'

Jeneba stepped towards me through the mist-covered heather. The mist furled around her feet like waves.

She was walking above the world, across an ocean of bright cloud.

'I can see for miles and miles,' she said. 'The mountains, they never end.'

'Try these,' I said. I tipped my binoculars out of their case. A small gold locket slithered out into my hand. It was

Sky Hawk

Iona's locket. It lay open in my palm, Iona's face smiling out at me.

And suddenly, it was as if Iona was with us there on the mountain. It was as if she had always been there. I curled my fingers around the locket and held it in my hand. My eyes burned hot with tears that wanted to come.

'Here,' I said. I put the locket into Jeneba's palm. 'My friend would have wanted you to have this.'

I turned away and closed my eyes tight, but the tears came anyway.

I'd promised Iona that I would look after Iris. I'd tried my best. A lifetime ago, Iona and I had sat on this hillside watching Iris fly over the loch and valley. And now I'd lost them both.

I jumped when Jeneba put her hand on my shoulder. 'Kulanjango . . . ' she said.

I turned to look at her.

'Kulanjango,' said Jeneba again. 'Look, Callum. She is coming.'

I wiped my eyes and stared through blurred tears. And there, above the sea of white cloud, flew a bird, its broad wings outstretched. It soared above us, its high call piercing the blue sky.

An answering call came from the mist in the valley below.

'Osprey,' I whispered.

It banked around and flew close, above our heads. I could hear the rush of air through feather tips. I knew it was Iris, I just knew it.

'She's back,' I yelled. 'She's back.'

I ran along the ground beneath her, my feet flying over the grass.

I spread my arms wide like birds' wings, and raced behind her, in her shadow.

She turned in flight and called again, 'Kee . . . kee . . . kee.'

And in that one brief amazing moment, her bright sunflower-yellow eyes looked right into mine.

ACKNOWLEDGEMENTS

Thanks to my fellow MA students and the staff at Bath Spa University, especially Julia Green for her tireless enthusiasm for the course. I am indebted to Nicola Davies for her insight and encouragement while I was writing this book, without whose help the pages would be overrun with sheep. Huge thanks to my agent Victoria Birkett, to Liz Cross and the team at OUP, and to Mark Owen who have created this book from my manuscript. Lastly, special thanks to Mum and Dad for standing in as head chef and head gardener, to my children for hiking across rain-washed mountains in search of ospreys, and to Roger, for telling me never to give up.

Much of my research about ospreys has come from the Highland Foundation for Wildlife (www.roydennis.org.uk), the RSPB (www.rspb.org.uk) and the Scottish Wildlife Trust (www.swt.org.uk). My inspiration for the Gambian part of this story came from visiting the website for the Bansang Hospital Appeal (www.bansanghospitalappeal.com). It is to the dedication of individuals in charities such as these that I owe this story, for having the passion and the courage to make a difference.

Gill Lewis grew up in Bath. For much of her childhood she could be found in the garden where she ran a small zoo and a veterinary hospital for creepy-crawlies, mice and birds. She secretly hoped a golden eagle would land on the bird table in need of urgent assistance. But it never did. Her favourite bed-time reading was *The Living World of Animals*. Gill followed her passion and studied Veterinary Medicine at the Royal Veterinary College, London. She has worked and studied both at home and abroad. In her travels she has been fascinated by wildlife; from urban foxes to rare rain-forest hummingbirds, and by the stories of the people who live among them.

Gill now reads and writes books for children. She completed an MA in Writing for Young People in 2009, and won the award for most promising writer on the course. She lives in the depths of Somerset with her husband and three children. She is still hoping to see that eagle.

COMING SOON

The sensational new novel by Gill Lewis:
White Dolphin

'The white dolphin is a sign that Mum's out there . . .'

When they first meet, Kara and Felix can't stand each other.
But on discovering an injured dolphin calf on the beach
they know they must work together to save it.

Now friends, they set out to find the truth behind
the disappearance of Kara's mother, and to protect
the nearby reef.

But powerful people don't want them to succeed. And
with the odds stacked against them, how can Kara and
Felix make their voices heard?

ISBN: 978-0-19-275622-0